THIRD WATCH PRAYER MANUAL

Geraldine Eddie McCann

Copyright © 2022 Geraldine Eddie McCann
All rights reserved
First Edition

PAGE PUBLISHING
Conneaut Lake, PA

First originally published by Page Publishing 2022

ISBN 978-1-6624-6743-1 (pbk)
ISBN 979-8-88654-207-3 (hc)
ISBN 978-1-6624-6744-8 (digital)

Printed in the United States of America

To My beloved parents, Annie and Charlie Eddie; my darling late, great husband, Robert; and cherished son, Robert Jr. (Robbie). (All of whom have transitioned to heaven)

To my loving sister, Vanessa, who was very instrumental in the publishing of this manual. To my nieces, Aquina, Shanaiya, Kashaiya, and Denira. To my nephews, Willie and Bernard Jr.

To all of my dear cousins, aunts, and uncles, including my loving extended family who I love and greatly adore, as well as my friends. Thank you all for always respecting, loving, and believing in me, you're the greatest!

To my incredibly amazing daughters and sons-in-love—Quanisha Lafrance' Latimore/Clifton D. Latimore and Yanisha Vontrice Minor/Carlton David Minor

To my cousin-son, Melvin Moore

To my fantabulous grandchildren—Gerice D. Latimore, Angel Dominique, Eddie McCann Jhaleel Anthony Williams, Robert Eddie McCann, and Gia Robyn McCann

Our dear, sweet beloved little blessing Gia, who passed through our lives on her journey directly back to her heavenly home. Gone but never forgotten.

To my dearest Mother Burrell with much love. You have been a great inspiration in my life for years. I appreciate your encouragement & Wisdom. I love you dearly. God bless you Mother & Stay Safe

Love
Sis McCann

Author's Note

God revealed this assignment during our 2020 (forty) day prayer and fasting consecration for the Lent season. One day, as my daughter Quanisha and I were watching the evening news, the anchor person mentioned that tomorrow was the beginning of the Lent season. My daughter exclaimed, "I can't believe it's almost Resurrection Sunday!"

I replied, "I know."

Then she said, "I wanted to go on a *fast*."

I quickly declared, "Me too!" What I didn't know at the time is that God was up to something far greater than I'd expected! Shortly after the prayer and fasting began, God began to reveal and unveil His *Third-Level Intercession Plan!* I honor Him for this awesome opportunity and privilege to be called and appointed by Him as one of *His third-watch watchkeepers*, covering the earth in intercession! Then the Lord, in His infinite wisdom, summoned my friend (who since then has become my spiritual daughter) Tameria Coley to join me on my quest to set the captives free! I'm so grateful to God for coupling me with a powerful intercessor. Tameria has great insight and wisdom! God uses her mightily, and I am so blessed to have her partnering with me in ministry. It has been a wonderful and productive prayer merger; I bless God in the highest for our union!

Preface

Much training has been given on the subject of prayer. Many of us have wonderful glorious stories to share about our prayer ventures with our heavenly Father! God has raised up thousands upon thousands of mighty and very capable qualified men and women of God, that have imparted an abundance of wisdom into us regarding prayer!

I respect every prayer giant that has gone before me, which makes me so honored that God has called me to share my prayer experiences that lead to the writing of this manual. My endeavor for you, as you read this manual, is for you to be inspired to increase your prayer-intensity. Prayer is such an awesome tool, not only against the enemy; it's a very refreshing and fulfilling opportunity to utilize your one-on-one access to God!

This book is not necessarily meant to teach you how to pray; however, it may certainly be a guide to those that don't have strong prayer practices! My prayer for the reader is to encourage you to explore and strengthen your fellowship with God through prayer! I promise you, if you pursue God, your life will be forever changed!

As your prayer and God-interactions intensifies, you will learn and experience the love and depth of His Heart on a level that you've never experienced before! It doesn't matter what prayer level you're on, God is ready to break bread with you through prayer! He is our awesome Lord that loves and adores us! Truthfully, He takes pleasure in building and expanding our relationship with Him!

> *Then you will call on Me and come and pray to Me and I will listen to you. You will seek me and find me when you seek me with your whole heart! (Jeremiah 29:11–13)*

> *You will pray to Him, and He will Hear you and will fulfill your vows. (Job 22:27)*

> *Therefore, I tell you, whatever you ask in prayer, believe that you have received it and it will be yours. (Mark 11:24)*

As you press into God, He'll press right back into you! God's love is unfailing! He doesn't just desire to hear from us when we're expecting something tangible from Him! He gets joy from daily fellowship with His children!

> *For the eyes of the Lord are on the righteous and his ears are attentive to their prayer; but the face of the Lord is against those that do evil. (1 Peter 3:12)*

> *I cried out to Him with my mouth, His Praise was on my tongue. If I had cherished sin in my heart, the Lord would not have listened; but God surely has listened and has heard my prayer! Praise be to God, who has not rejected my prayer or withheld His Love from me! (Psalm 66:17–20)*

Introduction

I praise the Most High God for this manual! My original intention for keeping notes were to record my consecration experiences; I was certainly not looking to write a book. God told me to keep a journal. I, myself, like to document my conversations with the Lord, especially when I am consecrating myself! I love to look back on my Godly dialogues and interactions! I love keeping a record of special seasons or moments in my life! Whenever God speaks to me, I consider it a profound experience!

God is completely magnificent. Little did I know, that when God told me to keep a prayer journal, that it would lead to the inception of this book! Even though God has downloaded several books into my spirit over the years, I've always known that they were books. As I continued taking notes, God kept manifesting His presence and revelation in such an awesome way, I quickly realized that this was much bigger than me! I now know that God had a greater purpose! These Godly downloads needed to be shared with the world, especially every prayer warrior!

However, I had no idea of the depth that God was taking me. All I knew was, during this 2020 Lent observance, this was a very different kind of *"seek for His Presence!"* I could feel this from the very first day. I love the Lord and have a strong desire to live in His presence. This is why I strive to live a surrendered life in Christ and that, of course, includes frequent fasting and prayer; I try to keep myself on His Altar! In spite of all of that, this was a thirst and undeniable yearning for God's *presence like none I'd ever experienced before!* The anticipation of an awesome fellowship with God was beyond exhilarating! This invigorating expectation began as soon as I told my daughter, yes to the consecration!

My prayer for the reader is that you too may experience the awesomeness of God on a level that you've never experienced before! Having Godly encounters on a regular basis is tremendously *awe-inspiring!* It makes for a bountiful and fulfilling life! His presence is so wonderful, till you have no idea of the joy that awaits you!

Acknowledgments

All praises, glory, majesty, and honor go to my heavenly Father for speaking this book into existence. Thank you, Lord, for every download, vision, and dream! Father, I bless You for all of the confirmations and revelations that you've given. God, I really bless You for the deeper-level call of intercession that's heavy on my life and for You using my life as an *end-time Watchkeeper"* in the third watch!

I'd been an intercessor since the early '90s but not on this level. Once I answered the call and accepted the elevation, my prayer life powerfully skyrocketed!

During the time of the fast, the Lord instructed me to keep a prayer journal. The journal quickly evolved into a book, from a book to the inception of *The Third Watch Prayer Manuel*. Thank You, Lord, for calling me into my purpose! Thank You, Lord, for trusting and anointing me for such a strategic task!

Father, I'm equally thankful to You for pairing me with an awesome prevailing Intercessory Prayer Warrior, Tameria Coley! Tameria's insightfulness in the Holy Ghost and continued prayer coverings have been an enormous blessing in my life! I can't give You praise enough for creating in the person of Tameria Coley—my prayer partner/friend/confidant and now spiritual daughter!

Tameria Coley

I want to thank you for recognizing and accepting the call of intercession on your life! Thank you for obeying the call of God to join forces with me; together, we combat the host of hell on behalf of God's people! Thank you for continuing to press into God, to receive the abundance of life-giving instructions, information, and confirmations that were essential to the writing of this manual! Thank you for every dragon you've slayed on my behalf and on the behalf of this prayer ministry! Thank you for keeping me covered in prayer, as I came under constant attack from the enemy!

Mr. Meyer Brown

I extend my sincere gratitude and appreciation to you for your kindness, understanding, and respect toward our prayer project. You've always been very patient with us; even during those times when Tameria and I have spent hours on the phone sharing and pressing into God's presence under the leading of the Holy Ghost! Thank you so much for sharing your wife with me!

Thank You, Lord, for Great Spiritual Leadership

To the late great Apostle, Betty Yancey

Thank you for shaping me into ministry. Thanks to you, I know how to battle in the realm of the spirit! Your intense teaching and preaching made me the woman of God that I am today! Thank you for teaching me what being a real Intercessory Prayer Warrior is all about! Now that I'm a mature woman in Christ, I can truly appreciate all of the difficult lessons and trials you taught me to navigate through! You most assuredly taught me to take a stand in the realm of the spirit, to stop running from the devil and to fight by submitting to God first and resisting the devil, so he can flee! I, now, have an awareness and knowledge on how to stand against the wiles of the devil and against the kingdom of darkness in Jesus's name! Lastly, one of the greatest lessons you taught me was that it is my God-given right to live a victorious life in Christ. For that, I will be forever grateful! Your teaching has left an indelible mark in my heart and a love, thirst, and hunger for the presence and knowledge of God. Because of you, it's deeply embedded in my heart! Rest on, Apostle, you've done a great work in Jesus's name!

GERALDINE EDDIE MCCANN

Dearest Pastor Carolyn Jenkins

Pastor Jenkins, I have so much to give God praise for concerning you! You have been a tremendous blessing to me and my family from the very beginning! You've been a constant source of encouragement to me, especially during my deep grieving period of bereavement for my husband and son! You spoke life back into me! You also prophesied to me that greatness will come forth out of me, after my grieving period was over. Thank you so much! You have always believed in me! You've always tried to thrust me forward—you never stifled me! You taught me the softer side of ministry! I can still hear you saying, "put some sweetening in it," when communicating with the people of God! You also taught me to be patient and understanding with the people, thank you so much! You never failed to exhibit love and kindness to me and my family. Pastor Jenkins, you are a beautiful, powerfully anointed pastor; great friend, and a greater woman of God! I thank God, in the highest, for allowing our paths to cross! Thank you for always believing in me, correcting me, and pulling greatness out of me and never, ever accepting mediocrity from me! I shall always love, honor, and respect you.

Archbishop William Hudson, III

Archbishop, you have been an amazing pastor, teacher, preacher, and father. I feel so blessed to know you! Thank you for every deliverance I endured at your hand. No matter the situation in my life, you always spoke directly into them through the Holy Ghost! I, especially, appreciate your love, kindness, and care given to me during my time of bereavement of my husband and son! I know, beyond a shadow of a doubt, that the Powerhouse Chicago was ordained by God for me to receive the strength and deliverance that I needed to get on the other side of grief! Thank you for every stern word that pushed me to my knees in prayer, pressing into God, for the more of Him. Thank you for every prayer rendered on my behalf.

Thank you for loving, trusting, and receiving me as one of your daughters in the Lord; I honor God so much for that! Thank you for the awesome sacrifice you made to receive such a powerful anointing on your life and for the miraculous power that flows and rests in the Powerhouse Chicago! I am forever grateful for the strong ministry connection that we have. I praise and magnify God for allowing me to grow by leaps and bound under your ministry! In short, Archbishop, thank you for everything! Thank you for every impartation and for leading me into the deeper things of God. I am forever grateful.

My awesome family

Thank you to my loving and supportive family for all the encouragement and prayers that helped bring this book to fruition! I give special thanks to my daughter, Quanisha, and son-in-love, Clifton Latimore, for always going the extra mile for me!

Quanisha, my firstborn

Thank you, my daughter, for being such a strong supporter of me; not just for this book but for many of my life endeavors! You've always been my go-to person! No matter what, you've always had my back. I thank you from the depth of my heart! Thank you for all of the encouragement that you've given me throughout the years! You're always the one that makes sure Mama and Daddy are good—I sincerely appreciate that! Even before your dear sweet dad went home to be with the Lord, you and Cliff have always been purposefully available! You both arranged your schedules to be conducive to our needs, making yourselves accessible to us; to date, you are yet doing that! So thank you for always looking out and making your parents a priority! I praise God for giving you the heart that you have. Not only does your heart reflect your godly upbringing, it also mirrors the attributes of your dearly departed grandmother and great-grandmother.

GERALDINE EDDIE MCCANN

Cliff, my son-in-love

Although, you're married to my number one daughter, you are truly a son to me! You have proven to both Robert and myself, over and over again, throughout the years that you possess the characteristics of a great son!

Thank you so much for all of your prayers regarding the completion of this book. Thank you for always speaking with great enthusiasm and belief about the success of this book. Thank you for always being a strong voice of encouragement and strength, which propels me forward with more of a determination to press through the obstacles onto the finish line! You, Nisha, and Gerice have been a constant source of support to me throughout the years. Man of God, I can't thank you enough! I will always be eternally grateful for you keeping the promise you made to our dear late Robert, which was to take care of me! He told you that he was leaving you in charge, you accepted the mission, picked up the torch, and never laid it down! I praise God for you, you're doing an *outstanding* job! It's been seven years and you, Nisha, and Gerice haven't missed a beat!

Yanisha, my baby girl

To my baby girl, thank you my daughter for all of the encouragement and love, not only for this book but in my writings throughout the years! You've always commented on the depth of my God-revelatory writings! It's a wonderful thing to know that, at an early age, God gave you the wisdom to realize that He'd anointed me to write! I remember back in the IHPD days, you always gave me great motivation as the Lord used me to write, even before I publicly acknowledged it! You've always spoken great words of inspiration into my life concerning that. I really, really appreciate it. It means the world to me!

Gerice, my eldest granddaughter and sidekick

Thank you, Gerice, my first-born granddaughter; for always being in my corner. Thank you for always standing up for your granny! Throughout the years, you've always encouraged and believed in me and making sure I am good. You are a beautiful granddaughter that shows genuine love and respect for me and for the anointing that's flowing in my life! I will forever praise God for you. You have a wonderful sense of humor and keep me laughing! Thank you so much for just being you—a beautiful young woman of God! God bless you, baby, and stay as sweet as you are in Jesus's name!

The Coronavirus

Now remember, at this time, the coronavirus was going on in Wuhan, China. In fact, I had been praying for them, but in all actuality, I didn't remotely think that it would hit the United States. And if by chance it did, I definitely did not expect it to hit at the magnitude that it did!

About four days into the fast, the coronavirus began showing up in the states! Of course, now, it's in my backyard. Therefore, now, I'm really purposefully praying against it in Jesus's name; needless to say, this virus has gotten my full attention!

The more I prayed, the worse the virus got! People were being infected and dying by the thousands all over the world! It was completely mind boggling!

I am an intercessor; therefore, I have an intercessor's heart! I cried out to the Lord in such disbelief as the death toll continued to mount! Oh God, why aren't things getting better, instead, they're getting dramatically worse? Needless to say, I am confused and distraught. My prayers seemed to go completely unanswered!

After the fourth day, I began to ask God, "What's going on?"

I explained to Him that I did not want to be praying against His will! I'd been rebuking the demon of COVID-19 to no avail!

The world was experiencing so much devastation, unlike anything I'd ever seen or heard of in my lifetime! Then immediately, God began to speak! God directed me to Revelation 6:7–8, *the opening of the (fourth) seal! When the fourth seal was opened, there appeared a pale horse—the spirit of death!*

> And when he had opened the fourth seal, I heard the voice of the fourth beast say, come and see! *And I looked, and behold a pale horse; and his name that sat on him was Death, and Hell followed with him. And power was given unto them over the fourth part of the earth, to kill with sword, and with hunger, and with death, and with the beast of the earth!*

Now, I have come to realize that this was part of the end-time woes, due to the world's rebelliousness and disobedience to God!

I was so grateful to Father God for revealing that to me! Then God gave me further confirmation by directing me to 2 Chronicles 7:14–15,

> "*If my people which are called by my name shall humble themselves, and pray, and seek my face, and turn from their wicked ways; then will I hear from heaven, and will forgive their sin, and will heal their land.* Now, mine eyes shall be open, and mine ears attentive unto the prayer that is made in this place!

I know I'm going against the grain by saying this, but every preacher that I heard talking about the coronavirus was rebuking the devil! Not once did I hear, let's seek God as to what's happening. They automatically assumed, as I did the first three days, that it was the devil! It's their belief that this virus came from satan! I don't know if it came from satan or if God sent it. God did not reveal that to me. All I know is that God allowed it! God sanctioned it! The enemy doesn't have that much power. God would not allow him to take over the earth and cause such devastation as if He is not God!

> *The earth is the Lord's, and the fulness thereof; the world, and they that dwell therein. For he hath founded it upon the seas, and established it upon the floods. (Psalm 24:1–2)*

This is God's world, and He hasn't given satan charge over it! Even if God hadn't confirmed it was Him, the saints ought to know that *God is God!* He is always in control! If it was the devil, the way the saints came together as a global unified body in prayer, rebuking him on one accord, it's no way he could have continued the destructive devices!

Prayer Shifting

God so shifted my prayer life! I no longer pray *emotional prayers!* I now pray *revelational prayers.* When we pray with revelation, we go into prayer with the knowledge and understanding that God has given, not what we think He's saying!

God's knowledge allows us to strategize! This type of prayer brings us into the awareness and in the complexity of our prayer-project! Therefore, we're better able to aim and shoot directly into our target and blow it up in Jesus's name!

Revelational prayers. Reveal and enhance our prayer life! As an intercessor, our heart is for the people! God gave me concise instructions and clarity which shifted my prayer objective. We must allow God to shift us as He sees fit!

Remember in 1 Samuel 30:8 how distraught King David and his men were after learning of the enemy's destruction of their camp and the kidnapping of their families! They dare not assume that they knew how to recover or even if recovery was available to them! They needed clear answers and directions from God of what strategic means they could use to retrieve their losses! After communing with the Father, He told them to pursue and that they would recover all! Glory to God! Just like God answered King David, He's waiting to precisely answer us!

When seeking the Lord, especially in intercession (the most selfless type of prayer), *we must always remain prayer focused!* The intercessor's focus should always be *souls!* Souls are God's most precious commodities! He said in Ezekiel 18:20 that *all souls belong to him! He said, the soul of the father as well as the soul of the son is his; but, the soul that sins, it shall die! God specifically and emphatically declared that!*

Consequently, intercessory prayer warriors, let's set our attention on souls turning and returning to God. God has taught me to attack the root-cause! The revelation that He has given me has totally revolutionized my prayer life! He has taken me deeply into a prayer search and pursuit for souls to be loosed from satan's grip!

As intercessors, it's a privilege for us to war for the souls that the enemy has in bondage! Our desire, as watchmen on the wall, is to help free the captives. It's our assignment to command and demand satan and his cohorts to lose them in Jesus's name!

There are so many souls hanging in the balance. So many souls trying to get out, but the enemy's grip is so deeply embedded in them that they require our intercession to help break them free!

As watchmen on the walls, we realize that no matter how hard we pray, so many souls will still be lost. That's why hell has enlarged herself to accommodate those that refuse to yield themselves to God!

> *Therefore my people are gone into captivity, because they have no knowledge: and their honourable men are famished, and their multitude dried up with thirst. Therefore hell hath enlarged herself, and opened her mouth without measure: and their glory, and their multitude, and their pomp, and he that rejoiceth, shall descend into it.* (Isaiah 5:14)

Unfortunately, countless souls will remain in eternal captivity; nevertheless, we must pray for those that God has assigned us to or their blood will be required at our hands (Ezekiel 3:18–21)!

> If you refuse to warn the wicked when I want you to tell them, 'You are under the penalty of death; therefore repent and save your life,' they will die in their sins, but I will punish you. I will demand your blood for theirs. But if you warn them, and they keep on sinning and refuse to repent, they will die in their sins, but you are blameless—you have done all you could. And if a good man becomes bad, and you refuse to warn him of the consequences, and the Lord destroys him, his previous good deeds won't help him—he shall die in his sin. But I will hold you responsible for his death and punish you. *But if you warn him and he repents, he shall live, and you have saved your own life too.* (Ezekiel 3:18–21 NLT)

God has a call on each of our lives! I'm not necessarily speaking of a five-fold ministry call. I'm talking about "a call to *serve* in our *assignment!*" We are servants of the Most High God. It's our job to help build His Kingdom in whatever area of ministry He chooses.

God gives us ministry keys to be utilized by us to accomplish His works. His keys will unlock any bondage that the enemy has His people locked in!

> *I will give you the keys of the kingdom of heaven; whatever you bind on earth will be bound in heaven, and whatever you loose on earth will be loosed in heaven!* (Matthew 16:19)

Chapter One

※

What is prayer to the believer in Christ?

Prayer, prayer, prayer, to the believer in Jesus Christ, is everything! Prayer to the believer is more than the need for water to the thirsty and food and raiment to the destitute! Prayer is life-sustaining communication with our heavenly Father!

Prayer is our lifeline! This lifeline connects and reconnects us to God! I remember a time when life existed without *cell phones*! Now, we live in an age where everything in this world seems to connect us through our cell phones! Now that we have them, we cannot imagine life without them! Well, the same holds true with our connection with God! Even though we treat our phones like a god, God is God, and He's God alone! Our relationship with Him should be much stronger, powerful, and more constant than any material thing on earth; nothing in life compares to His mighty presence!

Through prayer, we're able to maintain a lifestyle of obedience to God. It's the enablement of continual spiritual flow of strength and power that allows us to follow the teaching of the one true God!

However, in its simplest form, prayer is talking, connecting, and interacting with our God. Prayer is the process of giving and receiving messages to and from our beloved Father! Prayer is our means for healing and deliverance; we cannot live a prosperous life void of prayer! Prayer is talking to the only one that unconditionally loves us, no matter what mistakes we've made! Again, prayer is everything to us!

Prayer is our only means of communication with God. We can speak it, sign it, sing it, preach it, or teach it, as long as it's done in Jesus's name!

Prayer is not just having a discussion or an answer and question session with God; it's so much more! It's so much more, that if this book were entitled "What Is Prayer," it would never end!

There are so many thrilling and invigorating facets of prayer! Prayer stimulates and restores our minds! Prayer allows us to take a deep breath, even when life is being so hard-pressed against us! Prayer releases faith, strength, comfort, and peace into us! Prayer encourages and empowers us! Prayer quenches and satisfies the thirst and hunger for fellowship with God!

Prayer also allows us to feel the heart of God! Prayer enables us to know the personal God as a friend, father, mother, or loved one; whatever your prayer deficit is, He *is your supplier!* He will always listen and never betray us! Prayer gives us the ability to grow close to Him in a way that's unmatched with anyone we've ever met. Prayer is personal and very reassuring! If no one else understands, He always does! Please don't misunderstand, God loves us through prayer. Nevertheless, His love also corrects in prayer; please don't be mistaken, "He knows how to get us together!"

Blessed are those who hunger and thirst after righteousness, for they shall be filled. (Matthew 5:6)

Prayer is our bridge over troubled waters! Prayer brings clarity to unanswered questions! Prayer is our awesome tool of power and strategy! Prayer is our resource center for instruction, stability, knowledge, and wisdom; oh my God—prayer is everything!

> *If any of you lack wisdom, let him ask God, that giveth to all men, liberally and upbraided not; and it shall be given him. But, let him ask in faith, nothing wavering. For he that wavereth is like a wave of the sea driven with the wind and tossed; for, let not that man think that he shall receive any thing of the lord. A double minded man is unstable in all his ways.* (James 1:5–8)

Prayer releases and builds our faith in God. Prayer fellowship allows us to develop the characteristics and attributes of God.

Anyone who does not love does not know God; because God is love. (1 John 4:8 9 ESV)

> This is the message we have heard from him and proclaim to you, that *God is light, and in him is no darkness at all.* (1 John 1:5 ESV)

> Have you not known? Have you not heard? The Lord is the everlasting God, the creator of the ends of the earth. He does not faint or grow weary; *his understanding is unsearchable!* (Isaiah 40:28 ESV)

The fortitude of God is unrestricted to us as we spend time in His presence. His qualities are enlarged in us! These qualities permit His empowerment! Once we realize that we have the entitlement of God, we become resilient and resilience produces endurance!

Prayer allows one to die to oneself! Before Jesus went to the Cross, He died to Himself in the Garden of Gethsemane! In order for us to fulfill the will of God in our lives, we must first die to ourselves! We must get *that flesh together!*

Below, we will see the immense necessity for prayer regarding our assignments. *Jesus, the Son of God,* had to *pray* throughout His earthly mission. However, as He *approached* the end phase of His earthly assignment, He not only had to pray but His prayer *involved dying to His flesh!* The scripture tells us that He went and prayed three times; yes, prayer is a very necessary component of the life of the Christian! Moreover, Jesus not only accepted His assignment, there was never any doubt that He wouldn't complete it. He, just like us, needed the supernatural, enabling empowerment of His Father to get the job done, and we are no better (Matthew 26:36–41)!

1. Jesus said to pray that we don't enter into temptation! As we know, temptations come to pull us away from God's purpose for our lives!

2. Prayer will keep us alert; prayer also enables us to accept the hard assignments!

3. Prayer builds our Spirit man because the flesh is weak and ineffective to our spiritual assignments!

4. Prayer allows us to know the intensity of the assignment and the timetable or the expiration date for the completion of it!

5. Prayer helps us to continue *dying* to *ourselves!*

As you read these scriptures, you can see that they pack a big punch on the subject of prayer! With that being said, as believers, we have no other choice than to pray without ceasing (Luke 18:1)!

In—praying, it's most important that we pray with faith *(faith is the substance of things hoped for and the evidence of things unseen (Hebrews 11:1)!* Faith helps us to believe the seemingly impossible; *for with God, all things are possible (Matthew 19:23–60)!* Through faith, we have great expectations!

By faith, we receive access and boldness with confidence (Ephesians 3:17). We need these traits in order to walk in the fullness of God. People of God, that's great news! We have an all-access pass to the glorious provisions of God through prayer! We also have entry into His peace. His peace that passes all understanding that keeps our hearts and minds through Christ Jesus (Philippians 4:7)!

There are so many more benefits to prayer, that I can't begin to list them all! The intuitiveness of the Holy Ghost is an essential and tremendous advantage of prayer! Each time we pray, we achieve more perception and comprehension (Ephesians 3:18–19)! We also develop a closeness with our Father that keeps us rooted and grounded in love (Ephesians 3:17).

Prayer, also, keeps us renewed in the spirit of our minds (Ephesians 4:23). Prayer is everything to the believer! Prayer is a continual reservoir in our lives of ever flowing love, joy, and hope from our gracious Father through the name of our great redeeming king and Savior, Jesus Christ!

Prayer is as crucial to the believer as oil is to a car or as blood is to the body! Prayer increases our concentration and perseverance, which is a key element in dealing with the everyday challenges and stresses of life.

Prayer expands our problem-solving skills! Prayer gives us unmatched peace, contentment, and wisdom.

One might ask, how does prayer do all of this and so much more? Well, it's because we serve the highest exalted one!

> *The only wise God, our Savior; be glory and majesty, dominion and power, both now and forever! Amen! (Jude 1:25)*

His majesty, sovereignty, dominion, and power knows no bounds! He speaks all languages, and he speaks directly into every circumstance and situation with all knowledge and authority!

Jesus never changes!

> *Jesus Christ is the same yesterday and today and forever!* (Hebrews 13:8 ESV)

God is ever present!

> *God is our refuge and strength, an ever-present help in trouble!* (Psalm 46:1 NIV)

God is magnificent in all of His ways! As we lengthen our prayer fellowship with Him, we will find that each encounter with Him is an adventure! God releases vital life and satisfying nourishments into our spirits!

The dictionary defines nourishment as—food or a substance which is essential for growth, health, and good condition.

What this equates to is a prayerless life, an unhealthy life—naturally and spiritually so! This kind of life deems us powerless and makes us open prey for the enemy!

We need the supernatural empowerment of God to be physically and spiritually strong; which leads to a victorious life!

It's imperative that we remember, there is absolutely nothing too hard for God!

> Ah Lord God! Behold thou hast made the heaven and the earth by thy great power and stretched out arm, and *there is nothing too hard for thee!* (Jeremiah 32:7)

He understands everything and has all the answers; he's also very compassionate!

> *But you are a forgiving God, gracious and compassionate, slow to anger and abounding in love; the Lord is good to all; He has compassion on all He made psalm.* (Psalm 145:8–9)

> *When He [Jesus] saw the multitudes, He was moved with compassion on them, because they fainted and were scattered abroad, as sheep having no shepherd.* (Matthew 9:36)

Jesus saw the state of the people and how much they were in need of salvation, healing, and deliverance. His heart went out to them. We pray to God through Jesus. He is just as compassionate toward us as he was toward the people in the scriptures!

Those of us that have committed to an unwavering and purposeful prayer life are very eager to meet regularly with God! We wait with great anticipation to sit before Him! We are determined not to permit life, business, problems, or the devil's interferences and influences to prevent us from spending time in His presence! In fact, we are extremely grateful to God for loving us so much that He even desires to spend His precious time with us!

As fervent believers in Christ, we acknowledge that we spiritually die without His existence in our lives! Once spiritual death occurs, without repentance, it leads to eternal death!

Sin, when it is finished, it bringeth forth death. Do not err my beloved brethren. (James 1:16–17)

We know that all unrepented sin will take us to hell. That's why it's of great necessity that we spend time in prayer. The Bible tells us to draw near to God and He will draw near to us (James 4:8)!

We are rooted and built up in God (Colossians 2:7)! We have an established relationship with Him. When we allow breaks in our communication with Him, we truly miss our dear friend! It's similar to being in relationship with a natural friend. We love sharing and spending time with people that we love and have common interests with. We enjoy their company. Well, it's even more so with God! Our interactions with God, is much more rewarding than a natural friend because His love is one of a kind; nothing in life compares to it! God knows and understands all things, so there's nothing that we cannot dialogue with him about. He's the great…great listener!

As we express ourselves to God, through prayer fellowship, He manifests the joy, tenacity, and flexibility that we need to stand during the very difficult seasons in our lives.

We must remember that we are part spirit and part natural! We have not received our glorified bodies yet (1 Corinthians 15:44). Needless to say, it's crucial that we receive our daily connection with Him to maintain an exuberant life that ministers to us, the whole person!

Moreover, as we increase the pursuit of *prayer communion*, we shall undergo a rewarding transformation in our mind and our mindset that will thrust us forward and launch us onto a boundless level of trust, dependency, and belief in Him!

God is so ready to reveal and unveil His personal self to us! He has vital impartations and unimaginable secrets to unfold and unlock for us! On the other hand, this level of communication with God can only be obtained through *consistent prayer fellowship!*

Another very important factor is when we don't spend adequate time in prayer. We cheat ourselves out of experiencing the complexity of His glory!

Once you experience Him in this fashion, you become addicted to His presence! Your spirit requires and demands its regular dosages of awesomeness! Our lives are forever changed! *Mediocrity will no longer suffice! Once you've allowed yourself to explore and discover the deep waters of prayer, shallow or surface prayers will simply be inadequate!*

God is so good, and He is so faithful! He loves and adores us completely; therefore, He looks forward to our *godly interactions.*

As we spend time with Him, we obtain the steadfastness to conquer, defeat, and overcome on every trial level!

God's manifestations are so awesome and powerful. It's a very necessary component in our lives, especially during these end times.

We need the confidence and tranquility that's imparted into us as we seek Him daily. We realize that our everyday attendance with God gives us the assurance that He hears and answers our prayers.

> *And this is the confidence that we have in him, that if we ask anything according to his will, he heareth us; and if we know that he hear us whatsoever we ask, we know that we have the petitions that we desired of him.* (1 John 5:14–15)

Subsequently, I encourage (we) the people of God to establish and (or) reestablish and (or) enlarge and maintain a very meaningful and gratifying prayer-fellowship with Father God!

We're living in the middle of a pandemic, and the world seems very unstable right now; normalcy as we knew it is no more! *Nonetheless, Father God is yet in control! He has not gotten off of His throne! His majesty and sovereignty is still intact; glory to God! He still has supreme, dominion, and rule! With that being said, let's accept His affectionate invitation to spend quality time in His presence which calms, uplifts, and permeates our atmospheres in Jesus's name! Amen!*

As soon as we allow God complete access and entry into the very depths of our hearts—He will come in and sup with us. To sup with God means to commune with Him!

Jesus states in Revelation 3:20, *"Behold, I stand at the door, and knock if any man hear my voice, and open the door, I will come into him, and will sup with him, and he with me."*

God's written word is filled with His precious promises toward us. As we magnify our fellowship with Him, through passionate prayer, the words on the Bible pages will feel as if they've literally gotten off of the pages because those words are spirit, and they are life (John 6:63)! They have been greatly implanted within!

> *It is the spirit that quickens; the flesh profits nothing: the words that I speak to you, they are spirit, and they are life.* (John 6:63)

Our faith in God is increased thru consistent fellowship with Him. When we think about the magnanimous God that we serve, we should never enter His presence without first praising and magnifying Him. It is our job as His children to speak well of Him; speak well of the one and true God. For He is most deserving of all of our praises.

Praying in Accordance to God's Word

More very essential keys, before we can develop and ascertain a solid prayer-life, we must understand the fundamentals or the principles of prayer.

> Now we know, that God heareth not sinners: but, if any man be a worshipper of God and doeth his will, him he heareth. (John 9:31 KJV)

There is much controversy about this scripture; however, I believe the word as it states. I also believe in order for the sinner, or those that have not invited the Lord Jesus into their hearts as their personal Saviour, there is no assurance of answered prayers. Unless, it's a prayer of repentance.

God is such a great merciful Lord that I presume people, in general, sometimes confuse the extreme love and mercy that God has for the people, for Him answering their prayers. In this context, it doesn't mean that God doesn't hear their prayers. Of course, He does; He is the only wise God (Jude 1:26)!

Nevertheless, He hears but doesn't necessarily respond because He responds to those that He has a covenant with! A covenant is a conditional agreement between two or more people. A God covenant means that He has made an agreement with you to be your God, if you will be His people in obedience! However, the covenant or the agreement only works if all parties concerned do their part!

> But this command I gave them: 'Obey my voice, and I will be your God, and you shall be my people. And walk in all the way that I *command you*, that it may be well with you. (Jeremiah 7:23 ESV)

> *If you abide in me, and my words abide in you, ask whatever you wish, and it will be done for you.* (John 15:7 ESV)

When you come to realize the extraordinary magnitude of the benefit of having prayer access to our *magnanimous* God, it's selfish to expect that He is at our disposal! God is a holy God, and He expects holiness from us (1 Peter 1:16)!

Our carnal expectations of Him is for Him to produce for us, despite the absence or lack of love shown to Him or the daily faithlessness displayed and the total nonobservance of His deity!

We all have needs and desires that only the True and Living God can satisfy. Nonetheless, God has a set order! We must unequivocally love, honor, respect, and obey Him!

When we pray, we pray to God but we do it through Jesus's name! We cannot forego this process! We must adhere to the Word of the Lord! We cannot pray and get results without the acknowledgment of the *great sacrifice* that Jesus made for us on the Cross, while we were still sinners, through the shedding of His precious blood!

> *But God demonstrates His love for us in this while we were still sinners Christ died for us! (Romans 5:8 NIV)*

Once we believe and accept His awesome sacrifice, God renders us the distinct opportunity and guarantee of receiving answered prayers!

> *And whatever we ask we receive from Him, because we keep His commandments and do what pleases Him. (1 John 3:22)*

Despite what we may have heard or think, it's only one way of having the assurance that our petitions are granted, and that's through the power of the blood of Jesus Christ!

> For God so loved the world that He gave His one and only Son, that whoever believes in Him shall not perish but have eternal life (John 3:16 NIV)

Furthermore, I believe that there are some things God's going to grant us anyway. Not because we asked Him but because of His great love for us! Remember, He knows what we have need of even before we ask! It's understandable how an unbeliever can be confused in this area. When we pray and it comes to pass, we don't necessarily think about the processing of prayer. We're just grateful that our request was granted. It makes good sense, still God's word is His word, and His word is *truth!* The *eyes* of the Lord are on the righteous, and His ears are attentive to their cry (Psalm 34:15).

Now, please don't be misled or disheartened. God is a loving and merciful God. His mercies are renewed every morning (Lamentations 3:22–23). In spite of our misunderstandings, mishaps, or past failures of acknowledging Him, above all, He is a *forgiving God!* He doesn't hold grudges! In fact, He's waiting with outstretched arms, ready to receive all that wants to be received by Him! *"He says, whosoever will may come" (Rev 22:17).*

As a people dependent upon God, when we seek the Lord in prayer, we want to be in covenant with Him. *Knowing, with confidence, that help is on the way!* It's great to know that help is most assuredly on the way!

We were all once sinners, that are now saved by God's amazing grace! We all had to repent in order to be rescued from sin. God's grace is His unmerited favor toward us! *For all have sinned and come short of the glory of God" (Romans 3:23 KJV).*

There isn't anything we do to earn God's grace, we just receive it! He loves us so much until He just gives it to us! This grace allows us to acknowledge God and accept Him in our lives to be our personal Saviour! In doing so, we accept His gracious invitation and become His obedient servants.

> *For it is by grace you have been saved, through faith—and this is not from yourselves, it is the gift of God! (Ephesians 2:8 NIV)*

If you'd like to accept God in your heart to be your personal Saviour, it's quite simple. All you have to do is ask Him in, and He'll gladly enter.

Repentance is to be godly sorrowful for your sins and have a willingness, with determination, to turn away from them and to live your life by God's laws!

> *Repent* therefore and be converted, that your sins may be blotted out, so that the times of refreshing may come from the presence of the lord. (Acts 3:19 KJV)

Water baptisms: in accordance to the Word of God, we should be baptized.

Water baptism—to be immersed in water. Water baptism is an outward sign of the inward change that God has made in your life! This change involves the profession that you made to God, making the declaration that you no longer desire to live a life of sin! Thus, asking God to enter into your heart and save (or) rescue you from a life of sin! In other words, baptism is a public display of your new life in Christ!

> *Jesus answered,* "I tell you the truth, no one can enter the kingdom of God unless he is *born of*

water and the spirit [the Holy Ghost]. (John 3:5–7 NIV)

Flesh gives birth to flesh, but the Spirit gives birth to the Spirit. You should not be surprised at My saying, *"You must be born again!"*

Remission means that our sins have been completely paid for by the blood of Jesus! He hung on the cross and died for mankind's sins that we may be fully exonerated! Hallelujah, that's great news!

> *The soldiers nailed Jesus to the Cross; At noon the country became dark. The darkness continued for three hours—when Jesus died, the curtain in the temple was torn in two pieces. (Matthew 27:35,45,50 NIV)*

> For the sun stopped shining. And the curtain of the temple was torn in two! Jesus called out with a loud voice— *"Father into your hands I commit my Spirit!" When he said this, he breathed his last!* (Luke 23:45–46 NIV)

Receiving Salvation

Receiving salvation is really very simple. Basically, it comes down to your decision, to leave a life of sin and to live your life according to God's will. Now, you're ready to commit to God.

Furthermore, you are saying to God that you believe and accept that Jesus died on the cross for your sins and that He (God) has raised Jesus from the dead (Romans 10:9–10)! Now that you've made that confession—*the next step is to ask Him into your heart to save, or rescue, you from a life of sin.* This affirmation signifies that you are ready to surrender your life to God!

> *For the wages or the of sin is death, but the gift*
> *of God is eternal life through Jesus Christ our Lord!*
> *(Romans 6:23)*

If you're reading this book and have not asked the Lord into your heart to save you and pardon you from your sins, *now is a perfect time to do so!* Do you desire or feel compelled to give your life to Him? Are you tired of living a defeated and unfulfilled life? If you feel these words penetrating your heart—*please recite this prayer.*

* * *

Lord Jesus, I admit that I am a sinner, and I ask that You forgive me for all of my sins. I repent, acknowledge, and believe that Jesus died on the cross for my sins and that You, Lord God, have raised Him (Jesus) from the dead. I ask You, Lord, to come into my heart and save me so that my life will be forever changed. I receive Your love, and I ask that You cleanse me from all of my sins and wash me thoroughly from the inside out. Then Father, in Jesus's name, I ask that You fill me with your precious Holy Ghost with the evidence of speaking in tongues. Thank You, Lord, for saving me and rescuing me from the enslavement of sin. This prayer I pray in Jesus's name, amen!

*　*　*

Praise God—if you prayed that prayer in sincerity, you are now saved! Please be reminded—your salvation is not predicated upon what you might necessarily feel right now. You might not feel like your life has changed, but it has! You are what is known as a babe in Christ. You have just been spiritually born again. Now, you have to learn the ways of God so you have to grow.

Being born again means that you have died to your old sinful nature and have been reborn into the family of God! As your faith and trust develops in God, because of your profession, you will begin to experience the awesomeness of God! You have made a wonderful decision, the best decision that you'll ever make in life!

Hallelujah, God has freed you from sin! Please know that being saved is not being perfect! Salvation is a work in progress! Christianity doesn't mean that we don't make mistakes. It means that we no longer practice sin! When we make a mistake, we repent and with God's help, turn away from repeating the same error! *Now that you are saved*—it's imperative that you connect with a good Bible believing and Bible teaching church so that they may teach you the ways of God and answer any questions you may have about your new life in Christ.

As a new believer, if you don't have a church home, it's vital that you connect with one. My recommendation to you is an awesome church, the Powerhouse of Chicago, (773) 445-7600. You may call that number for further instructions and service times. Please tell them that Geri McCann sent you. Congratulations, my sister or brother, and welcome to the family of God!

It doesn't matter where you live (although, the church building might still be closed, as most churches are due to COVID-19); however, they have a great e-church online. The services are powerful and life altering!

The anointed leaders are, Archbishop William Hudson, III and Pastor Andria Hudson. You may look them up on YouTube or Facebook.

And I [God] will give you pastors according to [His] mine heart, which shall feed you with knowledge and understanding. (Jeremiah 3:15)

If you connect with this church, I guarantee, that once you apply the principles and teachings you'll receive, you will gain great knowledge and understanding about the ways of God. You'll grow by leaps and bounds in the Lord!

They are equipped with very capable ministers and a member services ministry, with members that are prepared to pray with you and to answer any questions you may have about your new found faith in God.

Growing in God through Fellowship

Building a solid relationship with God is crucial. This requires much effort on our part! The effort on our part involves navigating through the hindrances and road blocks of life and the devil! We know life happens to all of us. Our everyday life with our family, friends, and careers greatly occupy our time. That's why we prioritize our day by putting God at the top of the list!

It's also our responsibility to keep the enemy under our feet as he will never stop trying to trick us into falling out of fellowship with God! However, his power is broken off our lives; therefore, he cannot make us turn back, but he strongly and relentlessly tries! As Christians, we rely on the Strength of God to Stand firmly on and in His Word by studying and obeying; then we'll remain victorious and avoid the enemy's pitfalls in Jesus's name!

> *Finally, my brethren, be strong in the Lord and in the power of his might (Ephesians 6:10)*
>
> *Be sober, be vigilant; because your adversary the devil, as a roaring lion, walketh about seeking whom he may devour. (1 Peter 5:8)*

Please realize that we cannot do it in our own strength, but we can do all things through Christ who strengthens us (Phil. 4:13).

We get to know God through spending time in the studying of His word. This allows our faith to be cultivated. As we study His word, we learn to trust and apply the word to our lives so that we can flourish in the Lord.

ord here explicitly tells us that we must reach the heart of ... through faith and of course, our obedience to Him!

> *But, without faith, it is impossible to please Him; for he that cometh to God must believe that he is, and that he is a rewarder of them that diligently seek him! (Hebrews 11:6)*

Discovering the character of God

As we continuously read and apply His word, we discover God's character. We find that His character is that of pure love!

Everyone who loves has been born of God, whosoever does not love does not know God, *because, God is love* (1 John 4:7–21 KJV). *This is how God showed His love among us: He sent His one and only Son into the world that we might live through Him. God is love!*

Now that we're obtaining knowledge in the Word, we should be meditating on and memorizing the scripture. Our confidence is emerging; therefore, we have a greater understanding and respect for Him and maintain the importance of praise and worship!

Praise and worship are equally important as prayer! Praising and magnifying our holy Father is a wonderful display of our love, adoration, and appreciation to Him. Each time we praise and worship, we acknowledge His sovereignty and majesty!

God is the Almighty! He is worthy and completely deserving of all of our praises! We love Him and comprehend that there is no one like Him! We have come to know and believe that there is no other god that can save, heal, and deliver us out of any circumstance or situation! He is *the all-powerful one!* The Bible tells us that God inhabits (or dwells in the midst of our praises) the praises of His people (Psalm 22:3)!

When we praise and worship Him, His power pierces principalities and powers! Praise and worship are amazing weapons against the kingdom of darkness!

Our praises penetrate demonic atmospheres! Praise also releases reinforcements against the plan of the enemy. Praise also energizes, restores, and uplifts our spirits! *Praise is a dominant tool of defense and offense against the hosts of hell! Prevailing praise will break down satan's barriers of entrapments! As we send high praises to God—it opens the door for awesome worship!*

Worship

When we worship God, we bare our hearts to Him, and in turn, He bares His heart to us! Once this ensues—*an intimacy between you and God is established. That's incredibly undeniable!*

> *Yet a time is coming and has now come when the true worshipers will worship the Father in the spirit and in truth, for they are the kind of worshipers the Father seeks. God is Spirit, and His worshipers must worship in the Spirit and in truth. (John 4:23-24 NIV)*

> *Worship the Lord with gladness; come before him with joyful songs. (Psalm 100:2)*

As we open our spirits and pour out our hearts to God in love and admiration through worship, He makes exceedingly great impartations. These impartations can only be experienced and not explained. They are extraordinarily exceptional!

> *Come let us bow down in worship, let us kneel before the lord our maker. (Psalm 95:6 NIV)*

God is sovereign and majestic! He should always be esteemed very highly! Through worship, it is a wonderful means of reverencing His magnificence, which is unparalleled! Therefore, as He pours into us—He bares His heart by revealing parts of His personal self to us!

> *Yours, Lord, is the greatness and the power and the glory and the majesty and the splendor, for everything in heaven and earth is yours. Yours, lord, is the kingdom; you are exalted as head over all. (1 Chronicles 29:11 NIV)*

It's an honor and an enormous benefit to experience God in this manner! We deeply value His awesomeness and love that He has for us! The deeper you go into worship, you will find that His presence is tremendously breathtaking and rewarding! Please be reminded—God is a holy God, He is not to be toyed with! He will only receive true worship from a repented heart! It's crucial that we walk in holiness when we worship the Father! In other words, God is not asking us to be perfect. He's just necessitating that we admit when we've made a mistake, repent (turn away from it), and allow Him to forgive and restore us before we come to offer Him worship!

> *Therefore, since we are receiving a kingdom that cannot be shaken, let us be thankful and so worship. (Hebrews 12:28 NIV)*

> *If we confess our sins, he is faithful and just to forgive us our sins and to cleanse us from all unrighteousness. (1 John 1:9 KJV)*

Worship—cleanses and waters our spirits! Supernatural deposits are being made within us. Through worship, strategies are given to enable us to stand against the fiery attacks of the enemy. The resilience we receive from His awesome presence allows us to stand our ground and walk in authority over the enemy.

> *You, God, are my God, earnestly I seek you; I thirst for you, my whole being longs for you, in a dry and parched land, where there is no water. (Psalm 63:1 NIV)*

Worship empowers us to endure hardness as a good soldier of Jesus Christ (2 Timothy 2:3)! The oil of the anointing makes us pliable and flexible; we remain moist in Him, full of power and exuberant (not dry and brittle), powerless and defeated!

Worship is an intense love affair with our ever-loving Father! Worship gives us stamina and endurance! As soldiers in God's army, it's a requirement that we remain strong in the Lord and in the power of His might (Ephesians 6:10)!

Worship is a joyous God-fellowship that enriches us with the fulfillment of God's goodness that brings satisfaction and gratification on the maximum level; it's irrefutable!

> Therefore, I urge you brothers and sisters, in view of God's mercy, to offer your bodies as a living sacrifice, holy and pleasing to God—*this is your true and proper worship.* (Romans 12:1 NIV)

> *Jesus answered, it is written; worship the lord your God and serve him only. (Luke 4:8 NIV)*

Levels of Prayer

Entry-Level Prayer

As mentioned earlier, there are several levels of prayer. Many of you reading this manual may be new converts or babes in Christ and haven't developed a strong and consistent prayer life. If that's the case, praise God and welcome to the family of God! If that's not the case, maybe you've been in church for a while but haven't spent much time in prayer. I will say to you, it's certainly not too late to start building your God-connection!

Our God is a great forgiving God! All you need to do is admit to God that, for whatever reason, you haven't built a meaningful prayer relationship with Him. Once you do that, just repent, asking Him for forgiveness.

If we confess our sins, He is faithful and just forgive us our sins and to cleanse us from all unrighteousness!

Please be reminded, repentance is much more than just asking God for forgiveness. Repentance is asking for forgiveness with the willingness and the mind set of turning away from the thing(s) that kept you from obeying God!

For instance—if you are a workaholic and are too tired to pray, you must consider who blessed you with the job in the first place! You must cut down on your hours or make time in your busy schedule to have regular communication with God. Nothing in life is more important! We must make God a high priority. Sometimes, it's as simple as—just rearranging our schedules, putting God in the forefront!

Once you've repented, believe that you are forgiven because you are! Now, begin the enhancement of your relationship with Him. Make a conscience effort to start today—right where you are!

My suggestion is to begin with praising God, then the reading of the Lord's prayer as a guide into prayer. Praising God helps you become more comfortable as you enter into His presence. You will start to experience the joy of the Lord rising on the inside of you! Then you may start talking to Him from the heart!

Praising God before you enter into prayer is essential! As you praise Him, you are reminding yourself of the greatness of His glory and how blessed you are to serve such a matchless Savior!

Praise brings expansion to your prayer experience! As you praise God, He enlarges your depth in Him! Praise opens your spirit and breaks up the hard ground, making you ready to go into worship. Now, you're ready for an awesome prayer experience!

I praise you, God, my wonderful counselor, mighty God, everlasting father, prince of peace. (Isaiah 9:6)

Praise and Worship Are Equally Essential in Prayer

I praise God for the unexplainable *love* and *joy* that *floods our hearts* as we worship Him. The majesty and sovereignty of His presence and splendor makes our prayer fellowship an experience that penetrates our being. Nothing compares to it!

Worshipping God centers you directly in the heart of God! When you worship, He allows the heavenly rain to be poured in your spirit without measure!

My God—worship is such a powerful occurrence between you and our heavenly Father! Worship is intimacy with God! Worship is a manifestation of God's presence that all Christians should experience on a daily basis!

Worshiping God is an amazing overflowing joy that cannot be explained.

> *Come let us bow down, let us kneel before the Lord our maker. (Psalm 95:6)*

> *Worship the lord with gladness; come before him with joyful songs. (Psalm 100:2)*

Although we ask everything in prayer through Jesus's name, He achieved this honor by dying on the cross for our sins! He triumphed over the devil and received the esteemed privilege of transporting our prayers to God! Jesus accomplished a task that no one was worthy to undertake, and we are forever grateful to Him!

> *And when they were come to the place, which is called calvary, there they crucified him. (Luke 23:33 KJV)*

He was the only worthy and credible person to carry our sins to the Cross! He was without sin! God sent Jesus down from heaven to be born into this sinful world, to die on our behalf! Jesus is our great intercessor—always praying for us! Romans 8:34 states that Christ is at the right hand of the father, making intercession for us!

But God shows his love for us in that while we were still sinners, Christ died for us. (Romans 5:8 ESV)

For God so loved the world, that he gave his only begotten son, that whosoever believes in him should not perish, but, have everlasting life. (John 3:16)

For the wages of sin is death, but, the free gift of God is eternal life through Jesus Christ! (Romans 6:23)

We must always ask in faith, belief, and confidence! Faith comes by hearing and hearing by the Word of God (Romans 10:17)!

Faith: "But without *faith,* it is impossible to please him" (Hebrews 11:6).

Belief: "For he that cometh to God, must *believe* that He is and that He is a rewarder of them that diligently seek Him" (Hebrews 11:6–8).

Since Jesus Christ paid the ultimate price for our salvation and loves us with an everlasting love—we should desire and crave His presence. It should be our great pleasure to spend time with Him!

Remember, God so desires to communicate with us. He's genuinely concerned about what concerns us! As you develop a consistent prayer life, you will come to know Him as He'll reveal himself to you. You will grow in your trust and faithfulness to Him! Then you'll become exceedingly comfortable with talking with Him!

In Proverbs 3:5–6, it tells us to "trust in the Lord with all of our heart; and lean not to our own understanding. In all our ways acknowledge Him, and He shall direct our paths."

Trust, faith, and belief in God is a key factor in establishing a relationship with Him and in building a strong prayer life! As you commit to talking to Him on a steady basis, you will certainly get to know and love Him so much; His presence is totally awesome!

We must have faith that God is who He says He is and that He's able to do what He says He'll do, as long as we ask according to His will.

> *And this is the confidence that we have in him, that, if we ask anything according to his will, he hears us; and if we know that he hear us, whatsoever we ask, we know that we have the petitions that we desired of him! (1 John 5:14–15)*

> *Then you will call on me and pray to me and I will hear you. (Jeremiah 29:12)*

God is so good. Whether or not you have a condition or an incident in your life, it's always a perfect time to talk to our dear Father! It's an extreme blessing just to conversate with God, to become well acquainted with Him!

He will make life-changing impartations in your spirit, which releases unparalleled tranquility in your life!

> *Be careful for nothing, but in everything by prayer and supplication with thanksgiving let your requests be made known to God; and the peace of God, which passes all understanding, shall keep your hearts and minds through Christ Jesus! (Philippians 4:6–7)*

Next-Level Prayer

Now that you've become familiar with prayer and have experienced the joy of prayer fellowship, you've began to grow roots in God! The roots in God is Him releasing strength in you each time you plug into Him! The more you pray, the deeper your roots grow in Him!

> *And there shall come forth a rod out of the stem of Jesse, and a branch shall grow out of his roots: and the spirit of the lord shall rest upon him, and the spirit of wisdom and understanding, the spirit of counsel and might, the spirit of knowledge. (Isaiah 11:1–3)*

> *As you have therefore, received Christ Jesus the lord, so walk ye in him; rooted and built up in him, and stablished in the faith as ye have been taught, abounding therein with thanksgiving. (Colossians 2:6–7)*

Roots

Of course I am not, by any stretch of the imagination, a dendrologist or an expert in the study of trees. Nonetheless—I've always had an attraction and love for trees, I think they are amazingly beautiful!

We see trees every day; we also see their roots! Some of their roots are extremely long and thick; howbeit, they're much, much thicker underground! There is a particular tree named Methuselah. According to my research, the tree is nearly five thousand years old! It has very long, thick, healthy roots! The tree is located in the white mountains of California. It's an ancient bristlecone, a non-clonal organism—the oldest one on earth!

This tree has survived this long because its roots remain tough and resilient. This tree would not have stayed alive all these thousands of years without roots! Roots distribute the vital nutrients to the plants. Roots keep the plants stabilized above ground. Moreover, roots are the lifeline of the plants! Without healthy roots, the plant life cannot be sustained!

So is it in Christ. God gives us natural things in the world that are parallel with things in the Spirit! If we don't keep our prayer fellowship strong, our roots, which is our spiritual lifeline, will dry up and die! We need the vital nutrients of God's presence to not only sustain us but to assist us in growing thick, strong, and healthy roots in Him!

It is my prayer, as you read this manual, that you will be stimulated to enlarge your desire to experience God on a greater level! Also, that you will be determined to intensify your love, trust, and obedience to Him as you explore His magnificence through prayer fellowship!

Please be reminded—as you pursue Him, He pursues you! You must *draw near to God, and He will draw near to you (James 4:8)*.

When we choose to live our best life in Christ, even during the most challenging seasons of our lives, God's got us! He's our cushion! He will hold us with His powerful hands!

> *Now, unto him that is able to keep you from falling, and to present you faultless before the presence of his glory, with exceeding joy! (Jude 1:24)*

Be encouraged, saints, we've got much work left to do! Let's accomplish our assignments and complete our commitments in strength and power! Don't permit life's distractions to inhibit our progression in God!

Prayer is powerful and positive! Prayer is simply speaking to someone that loves and adores you, even though you may not necessarily be aware of the magnitude of His love toward you. Remember that He knows you and have been waiting to hear from you! God sincerely cares about you and any situation or circumstance you might be dealing with!

"God is love."

Matured-Level Prayer

Now that you've matured in prayer—by now, you've learned the importance of praise and worship before and during prayer. Praise and worship are mighty weapons against the enemy and an awe-inspiring boost into prayer! Praise and worship are the gateway into God's awesome presence! God is such a worthy God!

> *That it is a good thing to give thanks and praises unto the Lord and to sing praises unto thy name, o most high! To show forth thy lovingkindness in the morning, and thy faithfulness every night! (Psalm 92:1–2 KJV)*

> *I will praise thee with my whole heart: I will worship toward thy holy temple, and praise thy name for thy lovingkindness and for thy truth: for thou hast magnified thy word above all thy name! (Psalm 138:1–2)*

> *O worship the lord in the beauty of holiness. (Psalm 96:9)*

Oh, hallelujah, as you are now glorying in God's presence through *praise and worship*, you most assuredly understand why it is a prerequisite *and a key component of prayer!*

Praise and worship are very essential in softening our ground, moving our flesh out of the way as we make way into our God fellowship! Praise and worship breaks up our unplowed ground. It keeps our concentration on God and off the cares of life! When we seek God, we need to do it with our whole heart!

> *Sow righteousness for yourselves, reap the fruit of unfailing love, and break up your unplowed ground; for it is time to seek the lord, until he comes*

> *and showers his righteousness on you! (Hosea 10:12 NIV)*

As we praise and worship God, He sends blockages and stoppages into the enemy's camp that will destroy the distractions of the devil. These distractions will try to creep in and set up residence! The enemy's aim is to run interference in our praise and worship sessions to get us off focus. This is an attempt to prevent us from receiving the showers of blessings that is experienced during praise and worship.

Now, as a believer, the devil can't take our focus off God, but he can create a disturbance to entice us to break our concentration if we're not well-disciplined! As a matured level prayer warrior, the devil no longer has rule or dominion over us; therefore, we have the power to resist him and remain attentive in God! Once you have submitted yourselves to God, you have the power to resist the devil, and he will flee!

> *Submit yourselves, then to God. Resist the devil and he will flee from you.* (James 4:7 NIV)

A very wise woman and a former pastor of mine, Apostle Betty Yancey, once told us that "the devil will huff and puff—but surely, he won't blow our house down!"

> *For sin shall not have dominion over you: for ye are not under the law, but, under grace. (Romans 6:14)*

The grace of God is unmerited favor; you can't do anything to earn it. All we have to do is receive it. It's a benefit of His love for His people!

It's imperative that we walk in our authority! Yes, the enemy huffs and puffs but so what! We are on a committed level in God; therefore, we exercise our authority through binding and loosing!

Truly, I tell you, whatever you bind on earth will be bound in heaven, and whatever you loose on earth will be loosed in heaven. (Matthew 18:18)

Also, at this matured level of prayer, you should be at a measure of increased faith! We should understand that whatever we want or need from God is obtained by faith! We increase in faith by consistently reading, hearing, spending time in His Word, and doing or obeying His word!

So then, faith comes by hearing and hearing by the word of God! (Romans 10:17)

Another extremely good reason to obtain faith is we absolutely cannot please our heavenly Father without it!

We have trust and confidence in His faith!

And, this is the confidence that we have in Him, that, if we *ask* anything according to His will, He hears us; And if we know that He hears us, whatever we've *asked*, we *know* that we have the petitions that we have *asked* of Him! (1 John 5:14–15)

Now faith is being sure of what we hope for and certain of what we do not *see*. (Hebrews 11:1 MIT)

Additionally, we've learned that we believe God for answered prayers, period! We know that we don't have to see it with our natural eyes to believe it; we know that it is so! We've elevated to a degree that our desire is to truly *walk by faith* (2 Corinthians 5:7)!

Faith in God is everything! Faith allows us to build our love, joy, and respect for Him! We honor God because He's honorable! He's not a liar (Numbers 23:19)

> Then the Lord said to me, "You have seen well, for I am *actively watching over my word* to *fulfill it.*" (Jeremiah 1:12 AMP)

Deeper-Level Prayer Life

The Beautiful Ministry of Intercession

Intercession, I absolutely agree with those prayer giants that have paved the way for me to stand in belief of that. *Intercession is the highest level of prayer! Intercession is a selfless prayer. An intercessor goes to blows for others. We stand in the gap, subjecting ourselves and our families to insurmountable attacks!* It takes a special kind of person that will sacrifice themselves and their families in prayer for someone that they may not necessarily know! It takes a called-out person, anointed by God, for the mission!

As intercessors, the prime objective for prayer is to see others set free at any cost! Intercessors are in danger of taking the hits that's meant for those we pray for. Even though this kind of prayer brings us closer to Christ and is so rewarding, it comes at a high cost! We battle and do spiritual warfare on the behalf of people, regions, cities, states, or nations under God's Command!

Intercessors are responsible for numerous people obtaining salvation! We pray for many that we don't know and will never even meet! Nonetheless, we do it under God's command! We are confident of answered prayers because we're praying under God's direction! If God says pray for the healing of marriages, we know marriages are healed, whether we see it with our natural eyes or not! When He says to pray for worldwide salvation, we know that many are being saved!

Therefore, the job of the intercessors is to partner with God and go in the realm of the spirit and break up all blockages and hindrances that the enemy has set up to try and stop the people from yielding to God's beckoning! However, God doesn't need us to do anything because He is the Almighty! Nevertheless, He gives us assignments for those "hard-held" by the enemy in this earthen realm! He does this so that we can make an impact in the spirit realm! Our obedience to our assignment allows us, in the Holy Ghost, to put pressure on the enemy to lose his hold on those we pray for in Jesus's name!

As we go deeper into intercession, God's strategic level enablement gives us the upper hand on the enemy. We acquire these skills through living a life of frequent "prayer and fasting!"

Prayer and fasting

Prayer and fasting teach us to have discipline and to deny our flesh. When we deny our flesh in this way, we strengthen our spirit. We do this by not feeding our flesh what it wants in order to feed our spirits the word of God and prayer. We sacrificially abstain from eating natural foods so that our spirit man gets stronger and stronger!

Prayer and fasting also keep us praying in God's vein! Prayer and fasting release the vital empowerment to *hear, receive,* and *understand* God's prayer instructions. Remember, as intercessors, we aim to *precisely hit our target!* We want to hit the target with all the power force, in the Holy Ghost, to blow it up in the name of Jesus!

As intercessors, we battle all sorts of demonic spirits; we don't fear because of the love and protection of God! The Bible tells us in 1 John 4:18, *"There is no fear in love, but, perfect love casts out fear, because fear involves torment. But, he who fears has not been made perfect in love!" We are made perfect in the love of God! Therefore, there is no need to fear. God has us covered as long as we walk in His will. We can be unafraid because of God's safety and protection!*

We are His children. He loves, protects, and provides for us. In order for us to gain victory and know how to navigate in the spirit realm, we need the supernatural empowerment of the Holy Ghost to download into our spirits the necessary tactics to use against the enemy. Prayer and fasting help us to identify our prey. It also allows us to avoid mistakes, setbacks, and pitfalls as long as we follow God's leading. We are guaranteed the victory in Jesus's name!

> *Now thanks be unto God, which always causeth us to triumph in Christ, and maketh manifest the savour of his knowledge by us in every place. For we are unto God a sweet savour of Christ, in them that are saved, and in them that perish. (2 Corinthians 2:14–15)*

Deeper dimensions of prayer

Prayer and fasting help us break through the ceiling of surface prayers! What this means is, we break through the foundational barrier of prayer to go underneath the surface; this allows the heavenly portals to widen that we may go deeper in God!

We clear the passage of communication with God so that He may denote or warn us of any impending plans of the enemy! Make no mistake, the enemy is armed and dangerous as well!

Nevertheless, He is absolutely no match for God! God is our great Redeemer, and He is *Almighty!* There is no power stronger than Him! With that being said, we still must operate in the knowledge of truth! We ought not take the enemy for granted; we are no match for him without *the Holy Ghost!*

> Be Sober, Be Vigilant; Because your Adversary the devil walks about like a roaring lion, Seeking Whom he may devour. (1 Peter 5:8)

This scripture lets us know that the enemy hates us and will take every advantage over us not walking in wisdom! We praise God that *no weapon formed against us shall prosper* (Isaiah 54:17); nonetheless, we want to be well prepared for our opponent by being at the top of our game in prayer! Our objective is always—to set the captives free in Jesus's name!

We are confident that we've already won the victory; nevertheless, the enemy came to steal, kill, and destroy, and praise our great King that (Jesus) came, that we may have life and life more abundantly (John 10:10). Believe me, the enemy is always on his job!

Definitions

An intercessor—a guarded commander that uses their spiritual warfare keys to command and demand the works of darkness to cease in Jesus's name!

> *For this purpose the Son of God was manifested, that He might destroy the works of the devil.*
> *(1 John 3:8)*

Intercessors keep safe; we protect, we watch over and keep under close watch. We patrol in the realm of the spirit; we cover in Jesus's name! Intersession is not just prayer! We spiritually fight for the freedom and well-being of the individual, region, city, country, or nation we're praying for! We continue to pray until the burdens are removed and the yokes are destroyed! It is the anointing that destroys the yokes, and the bondage is broken in Jesus's name (Isaiah 10:27)! An intercessor goes before God in prayer to plead the case for others! Once the intercessor goes in, he or she gets strong opposition from the enemy while we're standing on the front lines in the line of fire!

Intercessors as guardsmen—fire diffusers! We keep order, we police, and maintain spiritual order! We make surprise attacks; we set ambushes and keep watch for sneak attacks of the enemy! We do whatever we need to do to cover and protect the ones we are interceding for. We stay submitted to God, as we spiritually fight in warfare, as we allow God's protection to cover us! It's crucial that we keep ourselves covered in Psalm 91 and Ephesians 6. *Psalm 19 reminds us of the goodness of God and also let us know that we are rewarded as we keep His statues!*

- The first level of spiritual warfare intercession is ground-level warfare! Ground-level warfare is the deliverance ministry; casting out devils (Matthew 10:7–8).

- The second level of warfare is against organized paganistic (or false religious practices), occultic worship, such as witchcraft and psychic reading; and so much more!

- The third level of warfare is strategic-level warfare! This level of warfare involves confrontations with high-ranking territorial demons. These demons have been assigned over certain territories to coordinate satan's plan of destruction of mind control over the people in a particular area. However, *Third-Level Night Watchmen are intercessors assigned to cover the night shift*. This involves Third-Level Intercession!

But, if our gospel be hid, it is hid to them that are lost: In whom the God of this world hath blinded the minds of them which believe not, lest the light of the glorious gospel of Christ, who is the image of God, should shine unto them. (2 Corinthians 4:3–4)

For we wrestle not against flesh and blood, but against principalities, against powers, against the rulers of the darkness of this world, against spiritual wickedness in high places. (Ephesians 6:12)

We are city defenders, gatekeepers, and officers of the night!

The purpose of an intercessor is to guard, cover, and protect those that we intercede for! Being an intercessory prayer warrior is a hard task—but a very rewarding position!

Intercessors are soldiers on guard in God's army! We maintain a defensive posture in the realm of the spirit! We stand armed, equipped, and alert, ready to war against the enemy on their behalf!

During this pandemic, as we are sheltering in place, this has been a great opportunity to commune with God and enhance our relationship and fellowship with Him!

As an intercessor—I count it all joy to stand in the gap for God's people! As we hear and witness so much suffering and misery in the lives of the people, our heart cries out! It's a deep hurt and you want to help! I feel that prayer and *intercession is my pandemic-contribution to the world! I know that I, along with my prayer partner, Tameria; are called to go in battle to assist in setting the captives free!*

Saints, let's remember, sin is the culprit—God is bringing judgment on the world because of sin! The devil is holding God's people in bondage through sin, trying to prevent them from breaking through—that's where the intercessors come in!

The intercessory prayer warriors, which are standing in agreement with God's will, are called to exercise our authority in Jesus Christ, to help set the deeply bound or the hard-held captives free! We prepare for the onslaught against the kingdom of darkness! Let's use every weapon in our spiritual arsenal, strategically, to free God's people in Jesus's name!

On March 19, 2020, a Perfect Prayer Union Was Formed

Again, unbeknownst to Tameria and I, was the wonderful spiritual journey that we were about to embark upon! We were unaware of the plans that God had in store for us. However, on Thursday, March 19, 2020, it began to unfold! On that day, I made what I thought was a random phone call to Tameria.

By this time, I'd moved to Minnesota from Chicago. We both belonged to the same church and served on the same ministry team. I was the team leader, and she was assistant team leader. After I left Chicago, we remained in constant communication because I continued to serve in the ministry as she transitioned into the full leadership role.

Although our friendship had developed by serving together in ministry, it flourished once I moved. God is so good! He quickly allowed our relationship to evolve from team member to friend from friend to coleader to spiritual daughter; thank You, Father! Even though we were friends, we hadn't spoken in a couple of weeks.

On this particular day, I decided to give her a call. When I called her, she sounded astonished! Once she answered the phone, I greeted her, then she replied, "Why did you call me?"

I thought to myself, *Because we hadn't spoken in a while, and I just wanted to talk to you!*

However, before I could respond, she began asking me, "Did God tell you to call me?"

I replied a resounding no! After that question, she went on to explain how the Lord had been dealing with her about joining me in intercession! I was elated! Tameria is a powerful Intercessory Prayer Warrior, a great asset to any prayer ministry! God knows I wanted her on my team. I wanted to ask her to join me, but I never felt the sanctioning of God to do so.

Tameria went on to say, today, as she was driving home from the church, she and God were having a discussion about Him telling her to unite with me! She was pleading her case before God as to why she didn't want to do it. She told God, no! She went on to explain to Him that she'd just come out of a five-month spiritual warfare battle and did not want to go back into that! Tameria was talking to Him as if He didn't already know her plight! We're all good for doing that! Don't we have a lot of nerve telling God what we will and won't do? Yes, we do! Nevertheless, we all do it and do it well. Forgive us, Lord, for we know not what we do!

However, what I love about Tameria's actions was that she surrendered her will to God! When we love God the way she does, He always wins in our lives! I believe we've found that He is not going to change His mind! He meant what He said and He Said what He Meant!

Shortly thereafter, she said I called her. Once I called her, she said that solidified it for her. She then asked to come aboard! Hallelujah! Although I was none the wiser, there could not have been a more perfect prayer union! We, through the awesomeness of God, complement each other in prayer! God, to this day, continues to confirm His formation of this union, and I am forever grateful! This is the day that God formed our Global Intercessory Prayer Ministry; Making UP The Hedge Prophetic Intercessory Prayer Ministry!

Midnight Revelations

At midnight, while in third watch prayer, the same day that God formed our prayer-union; God began to show us the demonic strongholds that's preventing the people from yielding or surrendering their lives to Christ.

God told us to pray against the pagan gods and the false religious spirits that governed the countries and regions. The ruling religious spirits were Islamic, Buddhism, and Catholicism.

Then the Lord showed Tameria an *octopus spirit!* She saw an octopus with the eight legs embedded into the heads of the people! The eight legs represented different groupings of spirits that governed different areas, regions, cities, countries, and nations! The Lord revealed to her that it was spirits of *mind control!*

We know that an octopus is a water animal that cannot live outside of it! We also know that the devil is a counterfeit and mimics the things of God! We realize that the Holy Spirit is symbolic to water. There are numerous scriptures to support that—John 7 is one of them, for example!

It's just like the enemy to assign a water demon to rule or control the minds of God's people! We've got to set them free in Jesus's name! The devil, in his wickedness, is trying to mock the Holy Spirit in unleashing that demon! As we go further, we will see that the enemy continues to assign water demons of destruction!

After Tameria shared with me what the Lord had shown her, the Lord told me how both revelations were in conjunction with each other!

The mind control starts at the head! The demonic influence from these false religious spirits had the people's minds confused! The enemy keeps tightening the confused screw into their mind and mindset! Therefore, they walk in rebellion and disobedience to God's will! They were incapable of understanding the truth! The Bible tells us to be transformed by the renewing of our minds (Romans 12:2)!

There were layers of demonic spirits to pray against such as deep-seated, generational spirits of doubt, delusion, unbelief, spiritual blindness, deception, lying, and false teaching. Moreover, *the ruling spirit is mind control due to false paganistic religious worship!*

The next night, Friday, March 20, 2020, while in prayer, God showed me what looked to me like a rat that had humps like a camel! As I researched it, I found that it was *another water rodent named capybaras! Capybaras are wild scavenger rodents! They can only survive if it stays near the water! It's, in fact, the largest water rodent in the world! Its size is in resemblance to a small dog! It can weigh up to 177 pounds; scavengers eat garbage!* This animal is a representation of the seriousness of the enemy's hold on the world! It also tells us how deeply embedded the enemy's grip is in the minds and mindsets of the people! God, help our people today in Jesus's name! This demonic spirit has nine brains and three hearts!

Here again, the devil uses a water demon! In fact, it's the largest water demon in the world, coupled with the spirit of mind control! As we can see, the enemy is not playing! The Bible tells us to be renewed in the Spirit of our minds (Ephesians 4:23). The sinner man cannot have the correct mindset as long as the devil has his mind confused!

Severed brain syndrome

The Bible tells us that as a man thinks in his heart so is he (Proverbs 23:7). We know that if a person's brain is scrambled and confused, the thinking will also be scrambled and confused!

> *But, I see another law in my members, warring against the law of my mind, and bringing me*

into captivity to the law of sin which is in my members. (Romans 7:23 NKJV)

I was praying to God about several horrendous acts of violence committed by an individual. I asked God to enlighten me on what causes someone to go on such a brutal and vicious killing spree. The Lord answered and said the person suffered from a condition called, *"Severed Brain Syndrome!"* Of course, I am not a medical professional nor have I ever heard of such a disorder, so I researched it.

According to the research, the scientific term for Severed Brain Syndrome is Split Brain Syndrome, which is a disconnection syndrome when the corpus callosum connecting the two hemispheres of the brain is severed to some degree.

This syndrome triggers a disruption with the connection between the hemispheres of the brain, *resulting in the patient displaying abnormalities!*

Brain hemisphere definition: cerebrum hemisphere is the part of the brain that controls muscle functions and also controls speech, thought, emotions, reading, writing, and learning. The right hemisphere controls the muscles on the left side of the body, and the left hemisphere controls the muscles on the right side of the body. Each hemisphere controls muscles and glands on the opposite side of the body, for example, the right side of the brain or hemisphere controls the left side of the body. The two sides of the brain are joined at the bottom by the corpus callosum. All brains have two hemispheres unless there is a birth defect. The cerebral hemispheres are divided right down the middle into a right hemisphere and a left hemisphere. The hemispheres communicate with each other through a thick band of two hundred to two hundred fifty million nerve fibers called the corpus callosum.

In my understanding, those suffering with Severed Brain Syndrome, the right and left side of the brain, are divided! This separation of the brain causes the two parts to work independently instead of working together. The brain operates as if there are two people living in one body! *Each part of the brain has its own abilities, instincts, and activities!*

According to what I read, when one split brain patient dressed himself, he sometimes pulled his pants up with one hand, that side of his brain's instinct said that he wanted to get dressed. And he pulled his pants down with the other hand, this side did not want to get dressed! Also, it was said that, once, this man violently snatched his wife with his left hand and shook her, so his right hand came to her rescue and grabbed the combative left hand.

Although severed brain syndrome is a medical condition, we, as prayer warriors, need to pray in depth when it comes to the "mind!" The mind is our information center; it needs to be clear in order to operate accurately!

Mental illness and personality and mood disorders should be thoroughly examined in the realm of the spirit! We realize that some conditions are medical, some are mental, some are personality-driven, and others or most, in my opinion, are demonic! It doesn't matter the origin, mental, or medical, both should be obliterated by the blood of Jesus!

We, the people of God, are servants of the Most High God. We better serve mankind when we're operating in God's wisdom! Why? *Because He is the only wise God. Our Savior, be glory and majesty, dominion, and Power, both now and forever! Amen (Jude 1:20)!* Things aren't always what they appear to be. Therefore, we search it out in God!

He'll tell us exactly what we're dealing with and how to approach it! It's just like I sought the Lord concerning the dreadful behavior of the man mentioned in the earlier chapters, and God answered! God is waiting to reveal hidden truths to us! Our archbishop, William Hudson, III, taught us that we are *solutionists!*

Our thinking concerning the enemy has been misconstrued! We sometimes underestimate his power. He is definitely not all power, nor does he have reigning authority, sovereignty, and rule. However, he does have some power and has no problem executing it against the people, especially the unsaved and the unlearned! We, as a people of God that's filled with the Holy Ghost, have rule and dominion over him!

Nonetheless, we must know our opponent and his capabilities so that we strategically arm ourselves as we get in pursuit of him! When we go after the devil, we must be equipped to go against the whole host of hell!

So let us walk circumspectly and in awareness, acknowledging that we indeed have an adversary—the devil that walks about as a roaring lion, seeking whom he may devour (1 Peter 5:8). What does that mean? Well, it simply means that he's coming for us! Well, yeah, he's coming for us as Goliath came for the Israelites! Goliath came with his suit of armor, his slew of demons. Glory to God, but we're coming for him with our five smooth stones—the Father, Son, Holy Ghost, our obedience, and determination; *in the name of the Lord Jesus Christ!*

Let's be reminded that *God is the Almighty, in Him we are always triumphant* (2 Corinthians 2:14)! *We are the victorious, more than conquering people of God!* We continue to bless Him for *His superiority, dominion, rulership, and amazing sovereignty!* So saints, let's get ready and remain in *position!* There is *much work* to *do!* In the voice of the late great Apostle Betty Yancy, "*It's our due season! So get off of our do-nothing stools and do something!*"

I believe when God spoke the name of this syndrome to me, He was telling me that because of sin and sin's bondage, the enemy was able to take advantage of the perpetrator's mind and used him against himself! This poor man was defenseless against the enemy's stronghold in his mind! Who knows, it could have been the enemy that caused the brain to split in the first place? *Sin took advantage of those commands and deceived me (Romans 7).*

    His unskillfulness in the Word of truth made him a prime target for the enemy! He also, most likely, was unaware of his medical/spiritual condition. If you remember, earlier in the book, I referenced that God showed my prayer partner, Tameria, the spirit of mind control and that the tentacles from the spirit were embedded into the minds of the people, preventing them from submitting to Him! This man is a very unfortunate prime example of that! He also represents so many others that's struggling with the same syndrome and other disorders just as detrimental!

For this reason, we must pray and partner with God in setting the captives free. We must stand on the wall with a hammer in one hand and the Word of God in the other! We must never come down! Nehemiah was rebuilding the wall in Jerusalem; the enemy kept trying to intimidate him to come down (Nehemiah 6)! God is using us, the people of God, to help build the kingdom of God, soul by soul! The enemy will try to convince us to move out of position through manipulation and intimidation or whatever deceptive device he decides to pull out of his bag of tricks! The devil knows that we belong to the all-powerful God and that he has no power or dominion over us, so he results to tricks! Nevertheless, we are committed. Like Nehemiah, we will not come down! We shall not be moved!

> *So the trouble is not with law, for it is spiritual and good; the trouble is with me, for I am all too human, a slave to sin. I don't really understand myself, for I want to do what is right, but I don't do it. Instead, I do what I hate! But if I know that what I am doing is wrong, this shows that I agree that the law is good. So I am not the one doing wrong; it is sin living in me that does it. I want to do what is good, but I don't. I don't want to do what is wrong, but I do it anyway! But, if I do what*

I don't want to do, I am not really the one doing wrong; it is sin living in me that does it. (Romans 7:14–17, 19–20)

If the enemy constantly fights the saint's minds to do evil, the sinner and the unlearned don't have a chance against him! Constant intercession on the behalf of the people gives them a better chance of accepting Christ than leaving them to discover Him on their own! We want them to come to know God as their personal Savior so that they may desire the sincere milk of the *word* that they may *grow!* After which, they themselves will learn the importance of making disciples of men! As we help build the kingdom of God, one soul at a time through discipleship!

Attack It at the Root

God told me to continue crying out to Him on behalf of the people but to redirect my prayers! Praying emotionally was praying against the devastation and the sufferings of the people, only without getting to the root cause of their sufferings! God loves us more than anyone can comprehend; nevertheless, He has to judge and punish sin and disobedience!

I was praying with a sorrowful heart because of the world's extreme distresses, instead of seeking God to know the reason for the sufferings. He taught me not to automatically think that it was the devil but to always seek His direction in prayer. That was a vital lesson learned!

Again, God said for me to seek to know the root cause of the world's anguish, then attack it at the root! In other words, God always want us to intercede for others. However, we must pray in His will; we cannot assume His will! His will is His word, and His word is His will! We must seek Him to know His will and direction! Once we have received His instruction, we have the missing element of prayer!

Not only did God give me a prayer strategy, He gave me the key component to getting answered prayers. Many times, things aren't what they appear! Sometimes, when we see world destructions, it's a result or reward for a certain world's behavior! It could be a penalty for what was sown! When we pray emotionally, it's easy to miss God's specific will in a situation! Missing His will could render very devastating consequences; it could make the difference between life or death!

Our goal as intercessors is to hit the *correct target!* We want to hit our target with all of the power and authority of God, completely obliterating it in the name of Jesus!

The intercessors have so much ground to cover in this earthen realm! We don't have time to pray haphazardly! It's imperative that we train ourselves to be super sensitive in the spirit so that we won't miss so much of God's messages! Don't get me wrong. Of course, we all miss His messages sometimes; nonetheless, we want to hear and heed His instructions more often than we miss them! God is waiting to unlock spiritual secrets to us! Sometimes, He'll release instructions, or He will give clues or allow us to take glimpses into the kingdom of darkness to give us an upper hand on the enemy's strategic plan! God will even completely unfold and expose the enemy's plan, if we walk closely enough with Him! All God-given information is beneficial and essential for the captives to be set free in Jesus's name!

God seriously ministered to me about prayer-aiming! When you aim, you are directing the bullets you shoot to destroy the desired prey. My cry to God about the world's suffering was surface. Surface prayers never get the roots! I was looking for a physical healing to a spiritual issue! The world is in dire need of salvation! There is very little benefit in putting a band-aid on a gaping wound! A physical healing from the coronavirus is good, but it's a greater gain to receive eternal healing!

Subsequently, God said, instead of me spending so much time crying to Him for mercy, spend the bulk of my prayer crying out for world repentance! Oh Lord, help the people spend time in intercession on behalf of the backsliders and the sinners yielding their hearts to You!

God totally shifted my focus! You see, everything that I was praying was correct, but my focus was incorrect because it was emotional. Emotionalism distorts our view and confuses our reasoning and vision! When we're in that state, we can become double-minded, which clouds our thinking! My prayers were completely centered around the hurting and dying people; I couldn't see pass that! Praying emotionally can cause us to hit and miss!

Many times, when we pray, we have to focus in on the root cause or the origin of the situation! Focus-based prayers are very advantageous, not only for the individual you're praying for but also for the intercessor or the deliverance worker! It also saves valuable time! When you focus or aim your prayers, you are praying strategically.

Strategic prayers teach us to search out the situation and not just pray what seems to be the obvious. In some cases, especially stubborn demons, it's vital to know what kind of spirit you're dealing with, whether it's generational, regional, or a ruling spirit. Once you get that information, it's more ammunition in your arsenal!

In other words, if a person has a debilitating disease, such as cancer, and they have a tumor, which is a growth, a symptom of the disease. In order to cure the individual from the sickness, the doctor knows that the chances of a positive healing outcome are greater if the tumor or mass is removed, then further treatment rendered! We must get to the root or the origin of the disease.

I'm certainly not a health care professional or a doctor; nonetheless, it makes no sense to treat the disease on the surface (the growth/mass) without doing further testing to get to the root—the source of the problem! Remember, our objective is to set the captives free!

It's crucial that we always pray in accordance to God's will! He always has a purpose and a plan! God is most concerned about the suffering in the land, but because of continuous disobedience, the world has tied His hands! God specifically speaks against sin throughout the entire Bible. God demonstrates His love for us and how much He desires to be our God; however, we must allow Him access to our hearts! He will be our God if we will be His obedient people!

> *But this thing commanded I them, saying, obey my voice, and I will be your God, and you shall be my people: and, walk ye in my ways that I*

have commanded you that it may be well unto you. (Jeremiah 7:23)

God has forewarned us about the consequences of sin. This plague is a result of sin! He told us several times in scripture!

That they may walk in my statutes and keep my ordinances and do them. Then they will be my people and, I shall be their God! (Ezekiel 11:20)

So the Lord sent a plague upon Israel from the morning until the appointed time, and seventy thousand of the people from Dan to Beersheba died! (2 Samuel 24:15)

God's tolerance for unrepented sin is *zero!* He has no relationship with it! You see, He had to bring judgment because He had spoken it! Since He cannot lie, He had to make good on His promise! *He even watches over His word just to perform it (Jeremiah 1:12)!* God destroyed Sodom and Gomorrah because of wickedness and sin (Gen. 19:24–25).

In these next pages, I will share some of the visions, dreams, manifestations, and revelations that God allowed us to experience as we're still being trained in third watch intercession.

Sunday, March 22, 2020

God showed me the face of an ancient-looking man! He was sitting in a sculpture bust position! Glaring at me! He kept changing in appearance from a black-sketched-looking portrait to a pale white-color, almost transparent looking! It reminded me of the Quaker Oats man but didn't look like him! He looked as if he was from that same era.

Then later after prayer (it was 5:00 a.m. when I woke up), I dreamt of what looked like a farm or a ranch that had a lot of children being kept and slaughtered! God later revealed the purpose of them being there, which was for devil sacrificing, breeding, and mutilation! Jesus! The ancient man I saw earlier represented satan!

Monday, March 23, 2020

Today, God showed me a man with his head down in his lap, with a perplexed-looking expression on his face! The Spirit of the Lord said to me that the relentless intercessory prayers were frustrating the devil! This, of course, gave us more of a determination to press forward, the more in Jesus's name!

Later that afternoon, when I spoke to Tameria, she had a similar experience! She dreamt that a dog was standing by her car, just glaring at her, the way the ancient man was glaring at me! She told me she knew it was the devil, but there wasn't any demonic character presentation! The devil transforms himself into an angel of light (2 Corinthians 11:14)! That's the spirit of deception trying to deceive us!

God is teaching us how to go deeply into the realm of the spirit! He's taking us to spiritual desert places of the earth and into the minds of His people, in order to unlock the captives from the bondage of mind control through intercession!

Monday, April 06, 2020

Earlier this afternoon, I saw a rhino's face with its mouth open in my face! A scare tactic from the devil—the devil is a liar! I rebuked it, got on with my day, and shortly thereafter, it went away!

In the evening, I spoke with my cousin Elnora Jackson, a powerful woman of God whose friend was awakened in the middle of the night by God hearing, "Earthquake, earthquake, and earthquake!"

Then later, during our third watch prayer time, Tameria saw Indians trying to create a storm and attempting to control the weather! God is so good! He allowed us to pray against the disruption of the weather and come against the prince of the power of the air! As intercessors, if we're connected to God's vein, we're spiritually connected to each other! It's vital that when God sees us, that He sees us a unified body! This is a great example of unity in the Spirit! It doesn't matter whether we are acquainted naturally as long as we've bonded in the spirit realm! When God speaks, we need to be ready to respond!

Tuesday, April 07, 2020

On this day—God showed me the devil unnoticeably mingling amongst the people! He also showed me Jesus or the angel of the Lord watching over the people as they went about their day. Then He showed me visions of babies. He showed me their state of being by their expressions! Their expressions included: sadness, pain, and despair! Also, God began showing me the state of the people in general *as they walked around! He ended the visions with the eyes of the lion! The eyes were the eyes of the Lord! The eyes of the Lord are in every place, beholding the evil and the good (Proverbs 15:3)! At the end of the prayer session, God showed me the most awesome sight! He showed me several flashings of scripture writings on my bedroom ceiling! I tried reading them, but they were moving too fast! Also, He let me know that the scriptures weren't for me, they were for someone that I was interceding for!* It was such a fascinating sighting! He told me that the adult person that we were praying for needed to hide the word of God in their heart so that they wouldn't sin against Him! He also said for the person to meditate on the word day and night! Another thing He said was for the individual to remain build up in Him by praying in the Holy Ghost!

The last glorious vision He showed me on this day were pictures of hearts and teddy bears on the ceiling. Then I saw a children's book, the cover had toys on it! God was assuring us that the child, that we were in deep intercession for, would come out of the traumatic situation well in Jesus's name! Amen!

Sunday, June 2, 2020

As I was ending my prayer, I saw satan's army assembling. They were equipped with their guns/rifles strapped to them! The army was bowing backward and forward! Then I asked God to explain to me what was He showing me? Then the demonic creatures appeared in the background. After that, I knew for sure that God was showing me satan's army! I prayed that God would increase or intensify the military-type protection around the intercessors in Jesus's name! I also pray that all intercessors will answer the call to pray; that they will cover all (eight) prayer watches! This is why the need for strong intercession is desperately needed on the battlefield; it's critical! Satan's army is armed, equipped, and ready to go!

Friday, June 06, 2020

God allowed me to see—demons' heads dangling from a rope from the ceiling. They were swinging in my face laughing! Then—I began to see many demons fighting against each other over territory! They're trying to steal ground from one another!

Prayer for man

As I pray for man, God stopped me and began showing me the state of the majority of men! He showed me the little broken, troubled, unhealed, bruised little boy living inside of man. The little boy that's trapped in the body of a man but incapable and unequipped to operate as a man!

Little boy-men make babies and obtain wives that end up in failed relationships! Those little broken, bruised, and battered boy-men produce after their own kind, and the cycle continues from generation to generation!

> *The earth brought forth vegetation, plants yielding seed according to their own kinds, and trees bearing fruit in which is their seed, each according to its kind. And God saw that it was good. (Gen 1:12 ESV)*

Men are the seed bearers, and this is the process of reproduction. Oh, but the devil is a liar. We break this vicious cycle in Jesus's name! We thank God for His power that He invested in us! We can bind together in the unified body of Christ and free our men through powerful intercession in Jesus's name!

God showed me a pleasant-looking little boy that still had his innocence! After that, I saw the pleasant little boy in man change into the hurt and disappointed little boy! Those two little boy-men grew up to become men without receiving the healing and deliverance that they needed! The boy-men's growth was stunted in the spirit, it was at a standstill! However, the body of the little boy-men grew into manhood in the natural! On the outside, the boys looked like men. Inwardly, they desperately needed inner healing and deliverance!

Father, in Jesus's name, we pray for the little undeveloped, unhealed, and immature boy in man! We pray for every boy that has had their innocence stolen from them. We release the supernatural healing enablement of God to completely deliver and restore them so that they may come into their potential as men in Jesus's name!

I pray for the damaged little boy in man! I come against the spirit of disparity in man! I pray for the disappointed and misunderstood little boy in man! I pray for the angry and scared *little boy* in man *that had no one to calm his fears!* I pray for every lonely, abandoned, and rejected *little boy* in man!

Oh God, we thank you for man! We thank you that every boy-man is made whole in Jesus's name! Man shall walk in total healing. Deliverance and restoration! Man shall walk in dominion and power! Because of man's wholeness, families will be restored and made complete in Jesus's name!

Sunday, June 13, 2020

While praising and magnifying God, I saw angels flying around! They had on white robes trimmed in gold. Praise you, Jesus!

Backlash and retaliation

Backlash and retaliation are real but so is the power of God! God's power will always prevail over the enemy! Always! Always! Tameria and I both have received backlash and retaliation from the enemy due to our nightly intense intercession! We have answered the call to be one of God's end-time watchkeepers and watch commanders! We have submitted to God; therefore, the devil always has to flee from us in Jesus's name. God always covers and protects us. He has given his angels charge over us to keep us in all of our ways! God even told me to feel free in using the number one angel, plus eleven more, that's been assigned to us in this assignment! These angels are, in addition, the host of angels that are available to the saints in general!

Therefore, we don't back down! We intensify our warfare! We must remain strong in the Lord and in the power of His might! We don't fear what the enemy can do to us; we trust God! We keep each other and our families covered in prayer! We remain in the whole armor of God! We try as much as possible to walk in forgiveness and repentance! Lastly, we keep all doors locked to the enemy.

I had an experience years ago! I literally saw a demon walk up the outside stairs of my apartment and stick some keys into the lock of my front door! It began turning the key as if it lived there! I could actually hear the rattling of the keys! I praise God that through the blood of Jesus, my doors are sealed shut to the enemy! Nevertheless, the devil is relentless in trying to get in any way he can! Of course, he tries to wear us down through trickery and deceit; he is yet a liar!

Not long ago, I saw in the spirit, a bloody female-looking witchcraft spirit standing outside of my front door! I first heard a knock at my door. I listened attentively; then, I heard the Lord quickly speak to my spirit that it was a demon spirit at my door! It was bloody!

Blood was streaming down both of its arms as they hung from its side. Blood was also coming out of every opening of the demon, the mouth, eyes, and ears! It had on what looked like a bloody burgundy-looking robe. As the arms hung down, the blood was pouring out from under the sleeves of the garment. As I watched through the peephole, I could see the expression on its face. It was the expression of innocence and fear! Then it said, while looking at me with its head slightly facing downward, "Can I come in?"

I replied with a *resounding no!* "In the name of Jesus, get away from my door!"

Now, we are aware that we are in control of our homes, spiritually and naturally. Therefore, the enemy will do everything to weasel its way into our house! Nevertheless, it's up to us to keep our houses protected in the Holy Ghost, through clean living and speaking the Word in strength and power!

Monday, June 22, 2020

I had a dream about intense warfare.

There was a man trying to emerge from what looked like a clear jelly-type solution! He was attempting to come out of bondage! As he stood upward, the devil grabbed him and entangled him again! We know that the Word of God tells us to *stand fast therefore in the liberty wherewith Christ hath made us free, and be not entangled again with the yoke of bondage (Galatians 5:1).*

There are many people of God stuck in satan's grip because they did not take the time to become strong in God! No matter what life throws at us, we need the strength of God! So intercessors, let's "go in" for them!

> *And the Lord said Simon, Simon, behold, satan hath desired to have you that he may sift you as wheat; but I have prayed for thee, that thy faith fail not; and when thou art converted, strengthen thy brethren! (Luke 22:31–32)*

Jesus is our perfect example of obedience, especially intercession. Romans 8:34 tells us that Jesus is at the right hand of God, making intercession for us! Intercession must go on day and night! God ministered to me about some of the weaker and immature saints that need us to keep them before Him, that they may walk in victory!

Friday, July 18, 2020

After praise and worship, I began seeking the Lord, regarding my prayer assignment for tonight. Then I see a little girl playing in what looked like a large puddle of water in the streets but near the sidewalk. She was sitting on the sidewalk with her legs extended in front of her while they flapped in the water.

There was a lady with her. All I could see was the lady's arms playing with the little girl's legs, but the Lord allowed me to know that it was a lady. Then the lady disappeared.

Baby—infantile, new, and inexperienced (water). They need the infilling of the Holy Ghost! The lady represented the intercessor—watching over and standing guard!

I praise God for giving me my prayer assignment to intercede for those that are in trouble and require our assistance breaking free in Jesus's name.

I began to pray for all of those that were babes in Christ, that they will acquire an unquenchable thirst and hunger for God that only He alone can fulfil!

As newborn babes, desire the sincere milk of the word that ye may grow thereby, but I prayed for those that are in bondage by satan's destructive devices; those that are stuck and cannot break free! *I also prayed for immature Christians!* I prayed for those Christians that keep making the same mistakes over and over because they are not walking in the fullness of God. Many of them are not filled with the precious Holy Ghost! I prayed for those that have been persuaded or lured in to believing the lie of the enemy! *I curse the spirit of beguilement in Jesus's name! I prayed for those that lack faith.*

Above all, *taking the shield of faith,* wherewith *ye shall be able to quench all the fiery darts of the wicked!* (Ephesians 6:16)

But, without faith, it is impossible to please him; for he that cometh to God must believe that he is, and that he is a rewarder of them that diligently seek him! (Hebrews 11:6)

The Lord told Peter, once he was converted to strengthen his brothers! Therefore, we have been mandated to cover and pray for each other, especially the weak, lost, and immature!

As I end my prayer session, I see another lady standing up holding a baby! I believe God is saying that we have to carry and hold some of the weaker saints until they're strong enough to stand on their own! We have to keep them before God!

Glory to God, I woke up that morning with a hallelujah song in my spirit. I woke up singing hallelujah!

Little did I know, Tameria was having a similar experience.

She said she heard an opera-sounding, angelic host singing in her ear! Thou shall not be destroyed! She said they kept singing it over and over! Hallelujah, praise God in the highest!

GERALDINE EDDIE MCCANN

Prayer against the Forces of Darkness

Father in the name of Jesus, I pray that you use your intercessors to create *cyclones* in the realm of the spirit against the demonic forces of hell! Father, we ask you to empower us to create *windstorms* and *tsunamis* in the kingdom of darkness. We speak confusion and disorientation in his camp every day in Jesus's name! God, we thank you for using us *to generate mudslides, earthquakes, and hurricanes* in the hellish realm! God, in Your authority, we *initiate disruption and interruption in* satan's plans!

Let the spiritual storms reek great havoc in his kingdom! God, *we shall root up, pluck up, and throw down his plans* in Jesus's name! We shall invoke massive disturbance and overthrow his schemes and plots in Jesus's name! We curse, cancel, and demolish every witchcraft incantation, hex, and vex in Jesus's name! We break, devour, and dismantle his wickedness! We release *the blowtorch, consuming fire of God to incinerate and devour* his tactics and destructive acts in the name of Jesus! Your lies no longer have merit! We destroy every tentacle and every fake pagan god in Jesus's name!

Your gods have eyes and ears but cannot see or hear; because your gods are fake, phony and powerless against the Most High God (Psalm 135:16; Psalm 115:5)!

God, we *thank You for anointing us for intensive-warfare!*

As intercessors and prayer warriors, we have the awesome opportunity to assist the people of God to break free of the enemy's hold! It's our job to guard, watch, and protect them in the realm of the spirit through intense prayer.

What Is Third-Level Intercession?

God is yet teaching us the meaning or the depth of Third-Level Intercession. However, in our experience, Third-Level Intercession has been intercession which requires a tremendous amount of *high-level and strategic-level prayer, coupled with constant communication and direction from Him.* This intercession assignment has been a step-by-step release of God's messages! Each night, it seems as if God releases another piece or two of the message puzzle!

In doing so, God has formed this global intercessory prayer ministry. God confirmed that He developed this ministry for the release of the hard-held captives! Third-level intercession is not only for individuals and families but also for the world and nations! However, as we know, this level of intercession keeps us completely dependent on God; it leaves no room for assumption. It's inconceivable for us to know our next move until He tells us! Third-Level Intercession also teaches us to rely solely on His leading! This level of intercession requires patience and stability in God. We keep our spirit man open to receive His vital downloads and communications.

Additionally, this level of warfare is not only exciting, exhilarating, and beyond rewarding; it explicitly teaches us undeniable discipline and trust in God! Even in all of this, we are just barely touching the surface of the depth that God wants to take us as we climb the global intercessory prayer ladder!

This level of prayer takes us directly into the enemy's camp! We go in strategically and prophetically! We strategize with the wisdom of God! Once we've unraveled the evil one's plan, we're in a position to receive heavenly instructions on how to eradicate his hold on the people! We go in specifically to disarm the enemy, dismantle his plan, and free the captives in Jesus's name!

As we pray, God allows us to operate in insight and foresight into the kingdom of darkness with the objective of practically praying and covering those we intercede for with knowledge and understanding!

During our prayer sessions with God, sometimes, His method of communicating our assignments or instructions to an assignment is done illustratively! Oftentimes, God will show me part of the nightly prayer assignment and show Tameria the final part without either of us knowing it at the time. We live in separate states and don't see each other often, so we don't find it out until we speak later after which the assignment comes together!

The necessity of us being super sensitive in the realm of the Spirit is unparalleled! The more we understand the operations of the enemy, the better prepared we are for a *successful retrieval of His people!* God allows us to peek into the kingdom of darkness to observe and educate ourselves on his many entries into the lives of His people.

I have been a called-out intercessor since the early '90s; however, never have I experienced a *prayer project* as powerful and rewarding as this one!

In addition to experiencing spiritual perception into the demonic realm, it has been our experience (Tameria and I), as we continue to dive deeper into intercession, that we're able to access heaven on a prophetic level! It seemed as if we'd hit a ceiling in prayer and then, broken through into the prophetic realm.

In this realm, God began speaking to us through illustrations and visions! He began showing us battles in the spirit realm. He even showed us the armies of the enemy assembling, ready to launch in attack! He would show us colors and pictures of strategies of the enemy. One day, as I was writing, I heard the Lord say, *"Third-Level Intercession." This is the first time that I'd heard this term!*

Oftentimes, He would show us so much that we'd have to search it out in order to get the message that He was conveying! Also, there were other times when He showed us clearly and precisely what our prayer topic should be.

We are very grateful and amazed that God has opened this realm up to us. We went from praying in English and in tongues to having dreams, visions, seeing pictures, and hearing words, names, phrases, and sentences in the spirit to hearing Him say, *Third-Level Intercession*. We are honored!

When God began shifting His communication messages to us, it was completely awe-inspiring! We are so humbled and appreciative of Him choosing us for such an assignment as this; we bless Him in Jesus's name!

Not only did He give us insight and foresight into the kingdom of darkness, He also revealed glimpses into the heavenly realm. He showed us angelic beings dancing and praising God!

He even allowed us to hear songs of praises being sung from our spirit man! We heard songs in English and songs in tongues coming out of our bellies. He is such an awesome God!

God also exhibited to us His anger and disappointment of His people. *He further allowed me to see His army assembled, strapped with their weaponry, and ready for combat!*

God is calling all intercessors on all prayer watches to get into position! God is calling us to work as a unified army! God has called me to cover the third watch and sometimes, fourth watch; this is where my focus is! It's imperative that all Third-Level Intercessors position themselves for third-level spiritual warfare!

God, being the mighty God that He is, went from dropping names and phrases into the spirit to giving names and paragraphs about the names He'd given! God conveyed to me when He releases the name of an individual, even if I'm aware of who that person is, I should pray and intercede for all that bear that name!

During the third-level prayer, God granted us sightings into the enemy's camp! We were able to literally see captives held against their will behind prison bars. He also showed us the spirits that held them in captivity. Moreover, God disclosed to us those that were bound in chains.

Furthermore, He revealed to us those that were being loosed from bondage because of our relentless prayers. God in His graciousness toward us unveiled the frustrated faces of the enemy due to the consistent powerful intercession that went up before Him on the behalf of His people.

God is so awesome. He enabled us to see the generational enslavement of the people. Then the Lord empowered us to annihilate the entrapments through the blood of Jesus in order to counteract the generational curses and to speak generational life, blessings, and wholeness throughout their lineages in Jesus's name!

This is why, sometimes, when we pray and pray and pray for people without any avail, the individual(s) really desire to come out of sin and sin's bondage but the generational pull of destruction that's on them. And their bloodline is too strong for them to break free on their own!

Some of these spirits have held their families into bondage for so many years until the enemy has convinced them that this is the way it is, and that salvation doesn't exist for them! *The devil is a liar!*

Therefore, it's our job as "Third-Level Intercessors" to go in and unloose the *hard-held captives and set them free in Jesus's name!* We have been mandated by God to go in and free them by the blood of Jesus!

God demonstrated to me that Third-Level Intercessors are a specialized unit in intercession, much like the Navy Seals are to the Armed Forces! What this simply means is that we have been called and trained in a deeper level of intercession, to unloose the hard-held captives from the entrapments and *deep enslavement and generational captivity!*

We do this by consciously and strategically following the leading and direction of the Lord! We do nothing of ourselves! All power and glory goes to Him! We live a life of much prayer and fasting! We train ourselves in the Holy Ghost to be super sensitive in the spirit realm. Our endeavor is to clearly hear, understand, and accurately respond to God's beckoning!

We also keep our ears close to His mouth to receive insight into the kingdom of darkness and to get an upper hand on the devil's schemes and plans!

Third-Level Intercessory Prayer Training

Please don't be misled, this level of training is not easy! It's actually very difficult, but it's extremely necessary for us to obey the call if we're going to win those souls for Christ!

Third-Level Intercession Training is ongoing! God is literally teaching us as we go! Sometimes, He gives us "on the job training!" Oftentimes, He'll give us a dream or vision first. He'll give us time to pray it through, but mostly, He releases revelation as He walks us through our adversarial encounters!

In the beginning of our training, God started by teaching us how to hear Him when He was speaking to us. We are yet learning the many ways of communication God uses to get His messages across. He's also teaching and training us how to appropriate and connect with what He is saying. That's why we continue to pray for super sensitivity in the Spirit. It is absolutely imperative!

Sometimes, it would be weeks in between God giving us pieces to the puzzle! We had to, first of all, learn to settle ourselves. We had to wait with the assurance that we heard God correctly and trust what we'd heard. After which, we had to dissect or pick His message apart, separating our thoughts from His message.

Now, we're in the process of allowing God to train our ears to hear exactly what He was saying and not try to make it make sense. We had to utilize patience while waiting with expectancy to receive God's revelation!

For example, He might show us a house. We would have to wait until He gave specifics about the house! Would it mean we should pray for dwelling places for the people spiritually and/or naturally? Or would it possibly mean for us to pray for a cleaning of their spiritual house! Therefore, we wait! If it's a spiritual cleaning that's needed, He'll most likely show us a dirty house with maybe some cleaning supplies in it. Since this assignment involves deep intercession, it's safe to say that if He shows us a house, there is a strong likelihood that deep inner healing is needed. It could probably mean a generational bloodline cleansing!

On November 30, 2020, I had a dream representing an unsaved man that I had been interceding for. In the dream, the Lord showed me a very large sandwich sitting on a kitchen counter near the sink. The sandwich was on the edge of the counter and partially on the sink. In the dream, I was cleaning up the kitchen. The kitchen had a double sink. The other side of the kitchen sink had some dirty, brown-looking food particles stuck in the bottom of it (deep-seeded). I began scrubbing it until I'd cleaned it up. After I finished cleaning the sink, I got ready to move the sandwich. As I got ready to pick up the sandwich, I turned to the man's wife, who was not paying much attention to me because she was leaving the house to take care of some outside business. However, right before she walked out of the door, I said to her, "Here, this is your husband's sandwich," as I attempted to pick the sandwich up to hand it to her.

She then stopped what she was doing and replied in a very stern authoritative tone, "I know it's his sandwich. Don't touch it, I'll get it!" She walked over to the counter and picked up the sandwich and left the house. Then I woke up.

The dream revelation was that God used me to go into deep intercession for the individual, through warring and travelling for his soul. However, I'd gone as far as God had determined I'd go. Although I was assisting in getting him clean and breaking the generational bondage off his family as a part of his salvation team, his wife had to bring it home! God also revealed that the stuck dark brown particles in the sink represented deep seeded generational spirits of blockages and stoppages of the enemy, which prevented not only him but his family from receiving Christ!

Also, God was telling me that the responsibility of the salvation of the woman's husband was on her, to stand in the gap for him and minister salvation for her husband. I am certainly not saying that this is always the case. On the contrary, most of the time, it's not. It was definitely not in my case! In this instance, God had given the salvation of this man to his wife to pray to fruition! That's why it's important to follow God's specific instructions. In the dream, God was showing me that I had a vital role in his salvation process, but the final step was to be completed by his wife!

God was also saying to the wife (which represents so many of us in today's busy world) to purposely and attentively be plugged into Him (God), to ensure we are on track with our assignments!

Even though we live in a fast-paced world, we cannot allow ourselves to get sidetracked! It's of the utmost importance that we slow the pace and make our godly assignments a priority! Our life situations have a way of wiggling in and distorting the scope of things, an enormous trick of the enemy!

In the dream, it was crystal clear that as soon as his wife saw me getting ready to touch the sandwich, she emphatically stopped me! Sometimes, we know our assignment but allow the cares of life to hinder the progression of it, even though we mean well. This man's wife was aware that her husband was her assignment! It was her job to push him all the way to the finish line. She, like most of us, needs to slow down and prioritize! Although this wife was already praying for her husband's salvation, she needed to fully focus her attention on it! Praise God. Once she did, shortly thereafter, he received Jesus Christ as his Savior! Hallelujah!

Of course, as always, prayer is definitely required; however, his salvation was predicated or linked, in this occasion, to his wife! We all must follow God's instructions if we want favorable results!

When we spend adequate time in the presence of the Lord, He'll teach us all things and bring all things to our remembrance (John 14:26)! God will show us our intercessory prayer role! Remember, intercessors, we all have one!

As an intercessor, it most assuredly gives us permission and the authority to pray for anyone, especially those that are in need of salvation. However, we all have a specific assignment, and everything is not assigned to us. We do well to remember that to prevent us from wasting valuable time or holding up progress! It's a wonderful thing to be led by God as He continues to commission us for the mission!

Deeper Dream Revelations

Jesus is Coming Back for a *church without a spot or a wrinkle!* That He (God) might *present it to himself a glorious church, not having spot, or wrinkle, or any such thing; but that it should be holy and without blemish.* (Ephesians 5:27)

Sitting on the edge of God

Sitting on the edge of the sink, and partly on the counter, depicts indecisiveness! He has one foot in and one foot out! The counter and the sink, both are surfaces that can hold him! However, one is a firm foundation, and the other is sinking sand (Matthew 7:24–27)! A lukewarm person that God will spit him out of His mouth (Rev 3:16). He hasn't completely given himself to God! He's on the edge. Meaning, he's not far from slipping backward!

This is very, very critical. Yes, he has come to God (praise you, Jesus), but his spirit needs much cleansing! He's on the edge because he's not completely sold out! Much, much strategic-level prayer is *required* on his behalf!

Dirty kitchen: represents the man's former state—his sinful nature!

Dirty sink: of course, represents the areas of deliverance he needs. The fact that I had to scrub to get it clean shows how badly he needs generational deliverance and how much I wanted it for him. However, God has specific plans and assignments for all of us. Simply put, he was my partial assignment! Also, God has me praying for him as well as covering her. *He allowed me to know that it was his wife's years of prayers coming up before Him on her husband's behalf that allowed the salvation process to begin.*

Dark, dried food spots.

Dried: the absence of moisture. Needing the moisture or the *oil* of the *anointing* flowing in his life!

The dark dried food spots also speak to the areas of deliverance that he needs to undergo! The fact that they are dried and stuck to the bottom of the sink says that they've been there a long time, most likely generational since birth!

The sink represents his old spirit man! It tells us that the spots have been stuck or lodged into his spirit, which makes them hard to dislodge but certainly not impossible! The dislodging or deliverance is made possible only through "the blood of Jesus" with hard-pressed prayer and fasting! This is "a this kind situation!" But this kind does not go out except by "prayer and fasting" (Matthew 17:21 EHV).

The large sandwich is his inheritance from Father God; however, it belongs to him because of the work on the cross. He is not yet in a position to be that sandwich. Meet for the Master's use (2 Tim. 2:21)!

The natural food in this context represents Christ who provides his spiritual food! This *food releases his life-sustaining vital nutrients that will keep his spirit man nourished and built up!*

> Jesus replied, '*I am the bread of life*. No one coming to me will ever be hungry again. Those believing in me will never thirst.' (John 6:35)

GERALDINE EDDIE MCCANN

Third-Watch Intercessory Prayer and Spiritual Warfare Training

In our preparation for intense warfare, God begins to train us. We began to have sleep deprivation like you wouldn't believe. There would be days, weeks, and even months when we would be so sleepy but couldn't fall asleep. There was a time when He had me covering both the third and fourth watches! I couldn't believe it! The training is *intense* to say the least!

As time went on, God would allow us to get a few hours of sleep here and there but never a consistent night of sleep for months! God was indeed breaking our flesh! It was extremely hard to cover those watches, especially dealing with extreme deprivation! Then God instructed me to study the US Navy Seals. After studying them, I knew exactly why the Father was doing what He was doing! He was getting us ready for the battles ahead! He was teaching us intense warfare!

Navy Seals

According to Wikipedia, the United States Navy Sea, Air, and Land (SEAL) Teams, commonly known as Navy Seals, are the US Navy's primary special operations force and component of the Naval Special Warfare Command. Seals are typically ordered to capture or to eliminate *high-level targets or to gather intelligence behind enemy lines!*

Navy Seals Training

The United States Navy Seals Training is immensely demanding, both physically and mentally. Its training is not designed to get you in shape. In fact, you must be in excellent physical condition and you must pass the PST (physical screening test) before you can be considered a Seal candidate. Not only must you be in shape, you must remain in shape!

The Navy Seals are named after the environment in which they operate—the sea, air, and land—which is the foundation of *Naval Special Warfare Combat Forces.*

Navy Seals are trained, organized, and equipped to conduct *a variety of special operations missions in all operational environments!*

The Navy Seals are an elite group of specialized warriors that are equipped in every area of combat! Their strongest area of warfare is the water (naval)!

Navy Seals Hell Week

In the beginning of the book, I talked about the water demons. God is preparing us to war against them by having us study the Navy Seals!

Hell week consists of five and a half days of cold, wet, and brutally difficult operational training on fewer than four hours of sleep for the entire week!

When we go up against the kingdom of darkness, we don't know what we'll encounter, but one thing's for sure, as long as the Lord of Hosts is leading the battle, *we're confident that we always win!* That's why we're humbled and honored to be chosen to serve in such a gratifying and rewarding area of ministry! I absolutely love the ministry of intercession because it is the ministry of healing and reconciliation (2 Corinthians 5:18)! Intercessors assist in reconciling the lost back to God!

God bless you, my fellow intercessors and prayer warriors, as you answer the call to pray. May you be armed for battle, focus driven, and positioned for warfare in Jesus's name, I pray, amen!

The end.

About Making up the Hedge PIP Ministry

In addition to the Third Watch Prayer Manual, Geri McCann is elated about the prayer ministry that Father God has also birthed in her: "Making Up the Hedge PIP Ministry." This ministry was birthed by God to lose the hard-held captives out of satan's grip!

For more information or if you have prayer requests, please submit them via email to makingupthehedgepipm@gmail.com. Thank you.

We have prophetic intercessors standing in the gap every Thursday. We fast and pray under the yoke-destroying power of God on behalf of His people. It's our privilege to see you, the reader of this manual, experience the chain-breaking, fire-anointing of God in your life and the lives of your family.

God bless you as you walk in the freedom of God, in Jesus's name we pray, amen.

About the Author

Geraldine McCann, better known as Geri, was born, raised, educated, and married in the city of Chicago but now resides in Minnesota. Geri was married for thirty-five years to the love of her life, the late great Pastor Robert L. McCann. To that amazing union, God blessed them with three wonderful children, two daughters and a son. In 2016, their only son, Robert Jr., transitioned to heaven. The Lord blessed them with five beautiful grandchildren, two boys and three girls. One of her granddaughters, Gia, also resides in heaven.

Geri has been saved for thirty-eight years. She's an ordained elder, a prophetic intercessor, and an author. She's been called, anointed, and appointed by God as one of His end-time watchkeepers. Her assignment is to intercede for the lost and to war spiritually to unlock their minds and their mindsets, especially the hard-held captives! She has gratefully and joyously accepted her mission in this earthen realm and is excited to see the breakthroughs of God's people.

CPSIA information can be obtained
at www.ICGtesting.com
Printed in the USA
JSHW060539210922
30774JS00002B/12